UNCONDITIONAL HEARTS

A MYSTIC BEACH NOVEL

ROXANNE HENSLEY

For Dwight, who has my whole heart unconditionally.

PROLOGUE

"*L*overs don't finally meet somewhere. They're in each
other all along."
    —Rumi

"YOUR HEART
    and my heart
    are very, very
    old friends"
    — Hafiz

"I WAS DEAD, then alive.
    Weeping, then laughing.
    The power of love came into me,
    and I became fierce like a lion,
    then tender like the evening star."
    — Rumi

*N*athan Scott paced in front of the mailbox, a decision weighing heavily on his mind. Would today finally be the day he unburdened the letter? He'd been carrying it around with him for a year, the toll noticeable in the folded-in corners and various indiscernible stains.

Was that coffee?

Standing in front of the mailbox had become a regular ritual, a tango rehearsed to the point of perfection. But the dance's ending needed work, since he'd yet to follow through with dropping the letter into the tiny slot. Would his duet with the mailbox include a permanent fermata before the final note, the big conclusion?

"This feels stupid," Nathan said, turning away from the mailbox for the third time that afternoon.

"Nate, what are you waiting for?" Frances asked. His aunt had joined him to ensure he actually followed through this time. She'd grown tired of the song and dance and was prepared to push the car into the garage, so to speak, if he ran out of fuel like he had for weeks during the ritual.

He sighed. "Sending a thank you note for a heart seems…

empty. Not enough. How am I supposed to truly convey gratitude for that?"

"One word at a time, I suppose. That's what you do—you're good with words."

His aunt was right. His very livelihood relied on word-smithing abilities. Having been a travel blogger for years, he'd never had a problem finding the right words to describe markets in Thailand, or the richness of Indian curry as it danced on his tongue, or even the sweet smell of ocean salt mixed with hibiscus on the lush island of Kauai. Even when snowflakes stuck to his eyelashes in Poland, he'd found an adequate way to express that experience with his readers and followers. But when it came to writing a letter to a family to express his deep gratitude for receiving their dearly departed loved one's heart in a transplant, he came up short. Everything he wrote sounded trite and shallow, falling short of expressing how he felt about having a second chance at life. What words were remotely adequate to sum that up?

Hence, the dance continued with the mailbox. Although he sensed his dance partner was growing tired from all the practice too, ready for the grand finale.

After the recovery, he'd reached out to his transplant coordinator, Lupe, asking for the donor family's contact information. She'd told him she'd be happy to pass along a letter, saying the family preferred anonymity. He tried using his charm to persuade her to share a name or location, but somehow, she was immune to his sweet talking and sexy smile. When that failed, he'd resorted to good old-fashioned arguing and then bargaining. But Lupe stood firm, passing along an address to which he could send the letter and guaranteeing it would reach the family.

"I still don't understand why I can't contact the family directly," he'd pouted.

"You are, by sending them this letter," Frances reminded him.

"You know what I mean." He rubbed the back of his neck, holding the pale blue envelope in his hand. The one thing he had charmed out of Lupe was that his heart donor was involved in a motorcycle crash, which validated his idea of two-wheeled vehicles being death traps. He'd imagined his faceless donor and the family he'd left behind in mourning too many times to count. Maybe it would provide the survivors with some form of solace to know part of their son lived on, providing Nathan a second chance, nay, a true first chance at life.

Having been born with cardiomyopathy after his mother contracted rubella during her pregnancy, he'd always been held back, handicapped from life's normalcy. He wasn't able to participate in sports like all his friends and always had a note to excuse himself from gym class. Sometimes, he'd puff up his chest when other kids wished they had his handicap so they could also be excused, but what they didn't understand was that Nathan hated feeling singled out. He wanted to be a normal kid and do normal things. But God made him different, irregular, instead.

It definitely didn't help when his mother disappeared shortly after he turned seven, leaving a note saying he was too much for her to handle. Overwhelmed at the prospect of being a single dad, his father had moved them both in with his sister so she could help raise Nate. Nate was particularly grateful they made the move after his father drank himself to death about a year after his mom skipped out on them. Aunt Frances certainly stressed to him how none of it was his fault, and he knew deep down that was true. But he couldn't help feeling partially responsible. Would his parents have made the same choices if he were born healthy? Nathan knew getting caught up in what-ifs was a worthless exercise, and he thanked God all the time for Frances and the fact that he wasn't alone.

Frances had been more like a mother to him than an aunt, anyway, leaving his broken heart filled with love. She never once made him feel like there was something wrong with him. She'd encouraged him to read instead of running outside with other kids in the neighborhood, hosting weekly book club meetings for two. They'd discussed the classics, his favorites being Huck Finn and Tom Sawyer. He admired their sense of adventure. He longed for adventure himself, dreaming about a world beyond his bedroom where he spent most of his time avoiding too much exertion. So, when he got the chance to get out there and explore, he went for it on a threadbare blessing from his doctor. Frances didn't agree with his choice, but she knew better than to argue. She knew everyone spreads their wings at some point, and he'd been cooped up for too long to continue keeping him caged.

And Nathan definitely spread his wings. He'd traveled to far off places, chronicling his adventures through a blog he'd started mostly for friends and so Frances could keep an eye on him. He'd gained quite a following, which led to sponsorships and endorsement deals until he actually earned a legit living from his adventures. He'd kept his heart condition a secret until it refused to stay in the shadows. He'd collapsed in the airport before a flight to Japan, earning himself a one-way ticket to intensive care instead.

The doctor told Nathan his biggest fear had come true—his ventricular assist device was failing, and he'd need a transplant. They'd short-listed him, but there was no guarantee he'd receive a new heart in time. He and Frances hoped and prayed together, and their prayers were answered while they were deliberating after reading the latest Jack Reacher novel. God was sending a heart from San Francisco to Seattle with his name on it. He'd finally be able to live and travel without fear or restraint for the first time in his life. He and Frances cried together, squeezing each other's hands before he went into surgery, promising to continue their book discussion after his recovery. It was the liveliest discussion they'd had to date.

And now he was expected to sum it all up in a simple, one-page letter.

"Nate, it's been a year. You need to drop it in the mail and move on with your life." Frances pulled out the big guns, resorting to good old-fashioned force as he waffled in front of the mailbox.

"You're right." He pulled the handle on the mailbox, balancing the pale blue envelope on the edge.

"Today," she nudged.

He let the handle go, metal slamming against metal, sealing his fate.

"Great. Now don't you feel better?"

Nathan shrugged. "I guess." He did feel like a weight had been lifted off his chest, breathing more deeply than he had in months.

"Now that that's out of the way, I've figured out a way to help with your other issue."

"Oh?" Nathan's ears perked up. His career had taken off in many ways once he'd recovered from transplant surgery. He was scheduled to attend and participate in a panel discussion at TravelCon in San Francisco where he'd also be meeting with a couple of network TV executives to discuss a new concept for a travel show. It was more than he could have ever imagined when he originally set off on his worldly explorations. More often than not lately, he needed to pinch himself to stay grounded in the fact that this was his new reality.

But there was one problem: he didn't know the first thing about negotiating a contract with television executives. Sure, he could handle negotiations for all-expenses paid trips to Tahiti or Tulum, but this was something completely out of his scope. He needed backup badly.

"Have I told you about my friend Coco?" When Nathan shook his head, Frances continued. "Well, she's in PR in Hollywood. Has been since we graduated from college many moons ago. I called in a favor, and while she's never worked with someone in your field, she does have relationships with the network your two executives work for, and she's agreed to help."

"That's great news," Nathan said. "Why didn't you tell me sooner?"

"One thing at a time. I needed you focused on mailing that letter." Frances's face turned stern. "And since we're on the subject, aren't you getting a little tired of living out of a suitcase?"

Nathan smiled. He knew where this was going. "No way. The spontaneity is what's keeping me young."

Frances elbowed him. "Come on, Nate. Don't you want to settle down? After all, I'd love to be a grandmother at some point before I die."

Nathan rolled his eyes. Frances made a habit of adding *before I die* to the ends of sentences lately, laying on thick whatever her agenda was, especially when it clashed with Nathan's. "Whatever. Technically, you'd be a great aunt."

"I already am." She grinned.

"No doubt." He smiled, wrapping his arm around her shoulders. "Come on, let me buy you dinner."

"Okay, but only if you're taking me to The Crab Pot."

"Deal."

ERIN PEDERSEN STARED at the alarm clock, anticipating its

signal to the start of her day. She watched time roll over, letting the clock cry out a few times to feel like it had done its job, although she hadn't needed it for quite some time. Sleep was increasingly hard to come by in the last month, let alone the last year. But she always set the alarm, just in case her sleep patterns went back to normal. She removed the body pillow from beside her, a cold excuse for the warm body who used to share her bed. She still hadn't grown accustomed to sleeping alone, but that wasn't the only thing contributing to her restlessness.

If someone had told her a year ago she'd return to Mystic Beach and take over her aunt Nancy's bed and breakfast, The Gilded Rose, she would have laughed them out of the room. But there she was, staring at an alarm clock as it blared its morning call before daybreak, telling her it was time to make the donuts.

Erin's aunt Nancy had been a natural born entertainer. She made friends everywhere she went, never knowing a stranger in her life. Erin even remembered vaguely how Nancy mused about owning a bed and breakfast someday after much encouragement from several people around her saying what a great hostess she'd make. Erin completely agreed, admiring Nancy's ability to charm a crowd, which was a skill she sorely lacked. Erin considered herself more of a numbers person than a people person. She'd even built a career in finance in what she now referred to as her former life, and it had been a struggle every day to play hostess. But Nancy had trusted Erin with her lifelong dream, and as much as her flight reflexes had kicked in, she'd forced herself to stay and fight instead.

She rubbed the sleep from her eyes before her feet hit the cold pine floor. Her toes recoiled in protest before she slid them into pink slippers, trodding down the stairs to brew coffee. She pulled her white robe a little tighter. Despite living in northern California her whole life, she'd never gotten used to the cold mornings. As the coffee brewed, she looked out a picture window above the sink in the butter-cream-colored kitchen, watching the fog roll in off the bay before the ascending sun performed its magic trick of making it disappear.

She pulled bacon and blueberry coffee cake out of the fridge before counting fresh eggs to make sure she had enough for her guests. She still wasn't used to preparing a breakfast spread every day. The morning routine in her former life had consisted of black coffee and a banana. She knew that would likely garner one-star ratings from the few guests that had booked their stay with her, so she channeled her inner Nancy, knowing exactly how she would want her guests treated.

When Erin was a little girl, she'd often wanted to stay over at Nancy's because she made the most beautiful break-fast spreads, with big fluffy egg casseroles, gorgeous fruit platters with all the colors of the rainbow represented, and heart-shaped pancakes with warm maple syrup. Cold cereal and OJ was the normal routine for Erin at that age, so staying with Nancy was a culinary treat she loved to indulge in every chance she could. But it was more than her amazing skills in the kitchen that drew Erin to Nancy's side. She always had the best advice, and if all else failed, solved prob-lems with warm bear hugs, which she gave in abundance to everyone she knew.

Needless to say, she'd left big shoes for Erin to fill.

She still wasn't sure why Nancy chose her to take over The Gilded Rose, since she certainly would never match her culinary skills, let alone the bear hugs. Regardless of the reason, she welcomed the opportunity to step into a new life after losing everything important to her in her old one. After Adam's death, everything felt hollow. She felt like an imposter as she moved through the motions without her partner in crime, which left her feeling incomplete. She still cringed every time she heard the rev of a motorcycle engine, silently saying a prayer that the rider would keep the shiny side up and make it home to their loved ones.

Adam had complemented her perfectly. He was the missing piece, the yin to her yang. He was bold while she was more calculated and risk averse. He lived in the moment, and she constantly assessed their future. He didn't know a stranger. Nancy loved him, naturally. And Erin was a wall-flower. Despite their differences, they'd loved one another with total abandon, accepting each other completely.

Even though it made her nervous that he rode a Triumph Bonneville T100, she'd trusted him when he said he was careful. She'd seen his care and attention firsthand the few times she hopped on the back as they rode through the streets of San Francisco, her stomach flip-flopping from more than the curves in the road. He was always responsible, never pushing beyond the limits of her comfort zone, which was a small window to maneuver through.

Based on his precision, Erin had a hard time believing it when she got the call. He'd been in an accident, a head-on collision with a truck, and was admitted to the ICU. After the call, things seemed to move in slow motion and fast forward at the same time as her grip on reality loosened. The medical team put him on life support, a machine doing his lungs' work while she waited patiently for him to wake up. But when he seized, she knew it was the end. Adam wouldn't have wanted to be kept on life support when it was clear his life was over, so she told the doctor in a forced staccato not to resuscitate. Her grip on reality dissolved, unable to come to terms with what happened as she clung to his lifeless body, sobbing for the loss of her true love. She never thought she'd have to face *'til death do us part* so soon. She was supposed to be frail and gray, not thirty-something and nowhere near menopause when death separated them. Part of her died along with him, a hole in her heart oozing pain, unable to clot.

It took a lot of time and mending, but eventually, Erin rejoined society as a mostly functional cog in the wheel. She returned to work, and after ten months, people were still giving her pitying looks, asking her if she was doing okay, touching her shoulder in a consolatory way. She knew they meant well, but she wanted to scream every time someone looked at her with woeful eyes. She needed a fresh start but wasn't sure where or how to get it. Then God answered her prayers in a twisted way through another death, this time her aunt Nancy, who left the inn in her questionably capable hands.

Erin didn't know the first thing about the hospitality industry or running a bed and breakfast, but she was determined to figure it out. After all, Nancy trusted her with everything she'd built, and Erin wasn't about to let her down. She considered herself a relatively smart person, and if she could manage the books for a large consulting firm, she could handle the books for a small inn. How hard could it be?

Erin smelled the bacon crisping in the oven and took it out before it burned. She cracked eggs into a bowl and added milk before whisking them together with a dash of pepper and salt. She'd learned firsthand how hard the balancing act of keeping guests happy and well-fed was, often shaking her head in wonder at how her aunt made entertaining seem so effortless. She hoped Nancy would at least nod in approval as her niece learned the art of innkeeping. Although she'd yet to wrap her head around proper marketing, and it seemed that was Nancy's Achilles heel too. With an average of thirty percent occupancy, money was tight. If things kept on the way they had in the last few months, it would be hard to keep the lights on.

Erin pushed those thoughts away from her mind, focusing on the task at hand of preparing breakfast for the four guests she currently had. Once the eggs were finished, she filled a carafe with coffee and placed everything in chafing dishes to keep warm until the guests were ready to eat. She sliced the coffee cake and put the pieces in a bread-basket before heading upstairs to put on something more presentable than her fluffy bathrobe.

After deciding to wait to shower and throwing on some clothes, she descended to the kitchen. Violet sat on a stool near the island, cup of coffee raised to her bow-shaped lips. She nodded hello to Erin, who was thankful she stayed on to help with cleaning after Erin had taken over for Nancy. She knew Violet's help wouldn't last forever, and even with money being tight, Erin didn't have the heart to cut her loose. Besides, she needed all the help she could get. Violet was studying music at Foothill College, and she'd likely transfer to Berkeley or San Francisco State once she earned her associate's degree. At least Erin didn't have to worry about that for another year.

If she made it another year.

"Grabbed the mail," Violet said, nodding with her frizzy blond bob toward a stack on the island next to her.

"Thanks." Erin filtered through the stack, hiding an enve-lope with Second Notice in red lettering into her back pocket. She knew what that likely entailed and didn't want to worry Violet. If she'd seen it, she had a hell of a poker face, as she was busy picking black polish off her fingernails.

"You know there's this magical substance called nail polish remover that does the trick in half the time."

"There's beauty in imperfection. I can't help that you don't understand my artistic expression." Violet grinned.

Erin smiled. "What's in the water over at that college you're attending?"

"Liberation from nail polish oppression."

Erin rolled her eyes and chuckled before telling Violet she'd take out the garbage. She took the half-empty bag and tied the drawstring, hauling it outside. She needed a moment alone to think. She couldn't hide from creditors forever and knew she needed to face the music. If she didn't find a way to increase occupancy, she'd lose everything her aunt spent her whole life building, subsequently tanking what little remained of her family's legacy in her hometown. She'd just hit the reset button on her life and didn't want to uproot it again.

She took a deep breath, forcing herself not to panic. Despite feeling completely out of her element, she wasn't ready to fold just yet. She had to see this through for Nancy.

2

*E*rin brought breakfast into the dining room and arranged the small chafing dishes on the buffet. She ran through a mental checklist to ensure nothing was out of place.

Eggs? Check.

Coffee cake? Check.

Bacon? Check.

Coffee and all the fixin's?

"Sugar and cream," Violet said, handing her the serving bowls.

"Mind reader." Erin smiled and placed them next to the carafe on the buffet.

"I'll start the rounds." Violet headed upstairs to start cleaning, passing an elderly couple on their way toward the dining room.

Erin greeted Mr. and Mrs. Abernathy as they shuffled toward her in matching yellow and brown plaid pants. "How'd you two sleep?"

"Like the dead," Mr. Abernathy said.

"Yes, the mattress is quite firm," Mrs. Abernathy said. "Good for his back."

"Glad to hear," Erin said, helping the two fill their plates. She ushered them to a table by a window overlooking the garden. "Coffee?"

Both nodded. "But hold the sugar; she's sweet enough already," Mr. Abernathy said. His wife giggled, playfully nudging his arm. He took her hand in his and brought it to his dry, cracked lips. Mrs. Abernathy blushed, brushing her free hand over the back of her perfect French twist.

Erin admired the spark of love still burning between the two septuagenarians. Her heart panged. She missed Adam in moments like these. She envisioned her and Adam ending up like these two, minus the matching plaid pants, of course, but life took a different turn. Her mind had barely begun to open to the idea that maybe, someday, she'd find love again. Not that she felt remotely ready yet. She had too much on her plate to think about matters of the heart. But whenever she *was* ready, she wanted someone who would look at her the way Mr. Abernathy still looked at his wife. She knew Adam would want that for her too.

"Here you go, lovebirds." Erin placed a mug beside each of their plates before leaving them to enjoy their breakfast. She straightened a couple of chairs at a nearby table, watching the Abernathys reach shaky hands across the table to fix each other's coffee how they preferred. They raised their perfect mugs and clinked them together before each taking appreciative sips.

Muffled voices coming from the foyer pulled Erin's attention away from the sweet moment. She rounded the corner to see a man with brown hair and a goatee talking animatedly to a woman whose blonde head nodded in agreement. What were the mayor and his girlfriend doing here? She hadn't seen them much since they both came to share their condolences right after she'd taken over the inn. True to their word, they both recommended The Gilded Rose to people passing through for chamber and city business, which she appreciated greatly. While their recommendations didn't always result in immediate money toward her bottom line, she'd seen an occasional uptick in bookings from the ripple effect of their generous word of mouth, their contributions helping her tread water.

"Marco, Elise." She greeted them warmly. "To what do I owe the pleasure?"

"Erin, so good to see you," Marco said, pulling her in for one of his customary greetings: a quick hug and a kiss on the cheek. "We wanted to stop by and thank you again. Our stay here a couple of months ago changed our lives."

"Yes, in more ways than one," Elise said, holding up her left hand adorned by a sparkling diamond solitaire.

Erin's face lit up. "Congratulations, you two!" She hugged Elise, then pulled back to take a look at the rock on her finger, a beautiful 2 carat round-cut adorning a white gold band. It fit Elise, who embodied classic elegance, perfectly. "Nicely done, Marco." She nodded her approval.

Marco's cheeks turned pink. "Thanks. That's not the only reason we're here. I'm not sure if you remember or not, but I was a good friend of Nancy's." He shook his head. "Again, I'm sorry for your loss. She was a very special lady."

Elise nodded in agreement. "From what I hear she always lent a helping hand to the Chamber and was such an integral part of the Mystic Beach community."

"Which is why we're here." Marco shifted his stance. "You may or may not be aware, but we've had several meetings lately on how we can drive tourism to our community. With how many people visit San Francisco, it would be fantastic if we were to lure a small percentage."

"Five percent," Elise interjected.

"Yes, even five percent would make an impact. Because more than likely, that five percent will tell their friends about the wonderful experience they had in our little coastal town, and we all know word of mouth is the best form of advertising."

Erin nodded, waiting for them to say more, but they stood in silence for an uncomfortable beat. "Makes sense to me, but what does this have to do with—"

"Oh, yes, sorry," Marco interrupted, touching her arm. "As I mentioned, Nancy was always supportive of our community's initiatives, and I'm hoping you'll help us with providing a room for a travel blogger for a few nights."

Just what she needed. Offering another room gratis to someone. If Nancy made a habit of offering rooms for free, it was no wonder things were a mess for the inn financially. Too many freebies and the whole thing goes caput. But Erin knew she was the new kid in town, and Nancy would turn over in her grave if she denied help to the mayor, let alone indicated things were dire behind the scenes. Besides, she had noticed a few blips on the radar as a result of the freebies. Although she wished it were more tangible than that, she had to take what she could get. It seemed her hands were tied. "Yeah, no problem. I would be happy to accommodate. . ."

"Nathan Scott," Elise said with a dreamy look. "Ugh, so gorgeous." Marco raised his eyebrow. "Sorry," she muttered, lifting the corners of her mouth at Erin.

He cleared his throat. "Anyway, Mr. Scott will be in town for a few days for a conference taking place in the city, and we've convinced him to stay here. In exchange, he's supposed to do a write-up on his blog about our town, and we're hopeful this will encourage people to make Mystic Beach their next vacation destination."

"He has quite a following," Elise mused.

Erin smiled at Elise's schoolgirl behavior. "When is Mr. Scott supposed to arrive?"

"Sometime today," Marco said. "Hope that's okay."

Thanks for the notice, she thought. "Yeah, I can make that work." She'd have to.

"Great," Marco said. "I really appreciate your willingness to support our initiatives."

"No problem." She forced a smile as she felt stress bubbling to the surface. She wasn't ready to have the inn under the microscope of a travel blogger's critical eye, but what choice did she have? And, seriously, people made money travel blogging? The world never ceased to amaze.

She began a mental checklist of the things she needed to accomplish before he arrived, and thankfully, Marco and Elise saw themselves out. She retreated to the kitchen to make an actual list before her mind cluttered to ineptitude. She took a deep breath as she examined the laundry list of tasks, not pausing to think before diving in.

With the Universe throwing her an opportunity for somewhat free advertising, she needed to make the most of it.

He'd dreamt about her again.

The bumpiness of the initial landing gave Nathan's heart a start as he touched down in San Francisco. He'd just woken from a nap where he saw her—a beautiful blonde woman with sparkly green eyes had made an appearance in his dreams as she had done for the last year. The dream was always the same. The woman held out her hand to lead him along a cliffside at sunset to watch the moonrise over the California coast. Her jasmine and amber perfume tickled his senses as he watched the early evening breeze brush hair from sun-kissed shoulders. Her hand fit perfectly in his, and he experienced an overwhelming jolt of electricity as her tender touch set fire to his skin. He'd stop her and his pulse would race as she turned to him, a burning question on his mind. But before he could ask it, he'd wake up.

The dream was identical every single time. She wore the same olive-green shirt and khaki shorts. Her blonde hair fluttered in the breeze in the exact same pattern. The sky was covered in the exact same pink and purple ribbons as the sun dipped below the horizon and night began its take-over. But every time, he woke up before he could ask his burning question, whatever it might be.

Nathan searched his memory for where he'd seen her, having no recollection of her unforgettable beauty. It had to have been somewhere during his many travels, but he couldn't recall a place or time, no matter how hard he tried. Her beauty was definitely memorable, and it bothered him when he couldn't place her. She had to be a figment of his imagination. His dream girl.

He was officially losing it. His mind had conjured the perfect woman and allowed her to haunt his dreams. He knew all too well the "perfect woman" didn't exist. In fact, he'd traveled to every corner of the world and never found her, thus proving his theory true. Frances' encouragement for him to settle down sure was manifesting in weird ways.

Nathan stood the moment the seatbelt light turned off and the plane had come to a complete stop. He waited in the aisle for his turn to de-plane and headed straight to grab his luggage from baggage claim. Normally, he traveled light with a small carry-on, but this visit required him to pack a suit for his panel discussion at TravelCon, which he'd been looking forward to for months. That and his meeting with the television executives who were interested in him for a new show on a travel network. He thought he'd better wear something nicer than his normal faded jeans and grunge band T-shirt. To say it was an important weekend for him was a severe understatement. This weekend would likely determine the direction of his career from here on out.

No pressure.

But before fate would unfold, Nathan promised the mayor of Mystic Beach he'd spend a few days exploring the idyllic coastal town and do a feature on his blog. He had to admit he was intrigued by the mayor's promise that Mystic Beach was the best kept secret in northern California, and Nathan had agreed to check it out. He'd never heard about the town up to that point, so the secret was definitely kept well. In all his travels to San Francisco, one of his favorite places in the world, it had never come across his radar. Better late than never, and the mayor promised to make it worth his while. In exchange for his time, he'd be staying at The Gilded Rose, a small bed and breakfast, for free.

"You're going to fall in love with Mystic Beach," the mayor assured him during their phone conversation.

"We'll see," Nathan replied.

He'd never fallen in love with a person, let alone a place. He preferred keeping his heart safely stowed away, locked in the upright position, free from turbulence. Of course, he'd had amazing experiences most people spent their lives dreaming about and often shared some special moments with beautiful women in all parts of the world. But eventually, he'd leave. Always alone. He doubted this weekend would be any different, although he was always open for a weekend fling.

But shouldn't he be keeping his eye on the prize? This weekend had the potential to be life-changing in many ways. He finally had a heart that could keep up with his wanderlust, and he was on the verge of getting everything he'd worked toward. He needed to keep his head in the game this week. The last thing he needed was a distraction, regardless of how beautiful she may be.

Nathan made his way to baggage claim and grabbed his suitcase, then headed to the rental car counter before hitting the highway toward Mystic Beach. He paused, feeling the sunbeams breaking through the clouds warm his skin. When he'd left Seattle, it was day twenty-six of cloud cover, and it felt good to bask in the glow. He rolled down the windows as he cruised through the city, taking in the salty smell of the ocean carried by the chilly breeze off the bay. His stomach growled as he thought about warm cioppino and freshly baked sourdough bread. It would be nearly impossible to narrow down his list of must-eat spots for this short trip, and at times like this, he wished he had hollow legs.

As Nathan drove, he realized something felt different this time. He felt a deeper sense of belonging, a homecoming which struck him as odd considering he'd always lived in Seattle. Now that he had a new heart, maybe he could move his home base. After all, he'd never intended to live in Seattle the rest of his life. Although when he thought about it, there was no way he could leave Frances behind. She'd been his angel all these years, the one woman to whom no one compared. The woman who saved his life. He didn't want to consider where he'd be if it wasn't for her. He owed everything to her, and Seattle was in her blood.

He exited the highway toward Mystic Beach and sensed an indiscernible shift in the air. His heart skipped a beat as he rounded a corner and caught a bird's eye view of the town of Mystic Beach nestled in a cove along the shoreline. Crafts-man-style houses lined cobbled streets winding up the hills, basking in the sun as it reflected diamonds over the bay. The ocean playfully sprayed boulders as waves crashed against the shore in steady rhythm, and he admired the colorful storefronts as he made his way through what had to be downtown. Families with strollers and growing baby bumps along with elderly couples with pretzeled arms adorned the sidewalks. He had to admit there was something magical about Mystic Beach. Why had it taken him so long to discover this idyllic cove?

The GPS told Nathan to turn right, and he wound his way up a small cobbled hill to find a weather-worn sign for The Gilded Rose. A cottage estate overlooking the bay, The Gilded Rose was the quintessential small-town bed and breakfast. Blue shutters framed each window with planter boxes overflowing with white hydrangeas and pink roses adding pops of color to the buttercream hardiplank exterior. A lush garden with an ivy and rose covered arbor and flint rock fire pit lent itself to special occasions and gatherings with picturesque views of the bay. He admired the meticulous attention to detail, feeling his heart beat faster as he drove around a circular drive and parked near the front door.

Nathan could hear the faint sound of waves crashing against the shoreline in the distance, and he paused to take it all in. He'd only been in town a mere moment, but already, he really liked what he saw. Upon entering the front double doors, he admired the crystal chandelier that greeted him in the foyer. The interior felt like stepping back in time, its opulence refined, yet cozy, reminiscent of an English country home at the turn of the century. The smell of coffee and bacon tickled his senses, and he wondered if he'd made it in time for a late breakfast.

"Checking in?" a woman asked.

Nathan turned to meet his greeter, his smile fading quickly. Shock followed quickly by confusion hit him as he gazed at his host. His heart fluttered in his chest, then leapt up into his throat. He felt faint.

"How—err…" He trailed off, completely at a loss for

23

words. He forced himself to take a deep breath as recognition set in. Her blonde hair was pulled up into a ponytail, revealing a delicate collar bone covered by smooth, ivory skin. Her sparkly green eyes met his gaze, seeming to penetrate to his soul and leaving him feeling exposed. She lightly bit her bottom lip, pulling Nathan's attention to her delicious bow-shaped mouth. The woman before him was easily the most beautiful woman he'd ever seen. But that was not what caught Nathan off-guard.

The woman standing before him was the woman *from* his dreams.

3

"*S*ir? Are you okay?" Erin's brow wrinkled at her new guest, who stared at her like a deer caught in head-lights. His eyes were the color of a stormy afternoon, and his clean-cut brown hair had just the right amount of salt and pepper to make him look refined. His five o'clock shadow added ruggedness to his strong jawline, enhancing his sex appeal. She had to admit it felt nice having a man stare at her, especially this handsome stranger. But when he didn't say anything, she felt self-conscious. "Is there something on my face?" She rubbed her cheeks and nose, wondering if part of the breakfast spread hadn't made it to the buffet.

"No." He cleared his throat and swallowed hard. "I'm checking in."

So, the mystery guest *could* speak. She held his gaze for a beat too long, feeling a shift in the air. Like the room suddenly held an electrical charge. Her skin prickled with goosebumps as she suppressed a shudder. Realizing she was the one borderline gawking, she broke the spell between them and walked toward the front desk. "What's the name?" She scanned her reservation book.

"Adam—I mean, Scott. Nathan Scott." He shifted uncomfortably.

Erin's heart squeezed at the mention of Adam's name. Her hand hovered motionless over the guestbook, and she almost dropped the pen. Who the hell was this guy, and what possessed him to say Adam's name?

Being an optimist, Erin wanted to believe in mediums or psychics who claimed they had contact with loved ones long past. But after going to several in hopes of making contact with Adam, she found they spoke in generalities that could apply to just about anyone or any set of circumstances, thus discounting their validity. But her fragile mind stretched to find a logical explanation on why this stranger would say Adam's name. Was this a message, a twisted prank from the great beyond?

She really needed to get a grip.

Erin quickly regained composure after taking a deep breath, avoiding eye contact with her guest as she pretended to study her book. So, this was the travel blogger she'd be entertaining for a few days. Elise wasn't lying when she said he was gorgeous. "Ah, here it is," she said. "I've got you staying for five nights in a king suite, correct?"

Nathan nodded. "Sounds right to me."

"You know, you don't look like a travel blogger," she blurted. She shut her eyes tightly. Why did she say that?

Nathan let out a surprised chuckle. "Oh? What do I look like, then?"

A GQ model came to mind, but she couldn't say that. She shook her head in embarrassment, her ears taking on a pink tinge to match her cheeks. "I—I don't know."

He smiled as she squirmed. "I guess I'll take that as a compliment."

Zing! There was that electrical charge again.

Erin grabbed the key to his room and handed it to him,

the current tingling up her arm as her skin grazed his. She caught a hint of his aftershave: sandalwood, orange peel, and ginseng. Her knees threatened to buckle. "Breakfast is served daily until ten am. There's plenty left, so help yourself if you're hungry." Her eyes locked on his, and she noticed specks of blue in his grey irises. She felt a spark of something else she couldn't quite put her finger on.

"Thanks, I may do that," he said.

Was familiarity that indiscernible spark she felt as she looked into his eyes? She didn't know how that was possible. She'd never seen the man before in her life. She'd definitely remember him if she had. Nothing about him was forgettable, especially his intense gaze and strong jawline.

Violet descended the stairs, breaking the spell between them. "Oh my God." She stopped dead in her tracks. "It's you! You're Nathan Scott." She almost dropped her broom. "I follow you on social media. I love your posts."

His face flushed from Violet's fangirl behavior. "Thank you."

"Are you here for TravelCon?" Violet asked, and he nodded. "That's so cool." She beamed.

"I guess I'll go get settled in," he said.

"Your room is upstairs down the hall to the left," Erin said.

"Thanks." He picked up his bag and headed upstairs. He smiled at Violet as he passed her, and Violet mimicked a silent scream toward Erin. Erin smiled, motioning for Violet to come down to talk to her.

"Oh my God. It's so cool that he's here," Violet gushed when she approached Erin.

"You know who he is?"

"Uh, yeah. He's one of the most influential travel bloggers in the world, *and* he's hot. He occasionally posts shirtless pictures of himself around the world, and let's just say I've added some random locations to my must visit list after seeing his posts."

Erin smiled. "I had no idea you were so interested in travel."

"He makes it interesting."

Erin chuckled. "I see."

"I can't believe you didn't tell me he was coming." Violet playfully elbowed her.

Erin shrugged. "I didn't realize he was such a big deal. Besides, don't *famous* people tend to like their privacy?" She couldn't help saying the word famous with a bit of a slant. She'd never understood the obsession with celebrities. They were regular people who just happened to have a talent very few other people possessed, but they were human, none-theless.

"He forfeited his privacy once he became an influencer," Violet said.

Erin snorted. She still couldn't wrap her head around the whole social media stardom phenomenon. Since when did posting pictures of eating food in far off places constitute talent? She didn't think most people really cared about that stuff, and here she had a guest who made a living doing that exact thing, and an innkeeper fan-girling over him. She shook her head at the thought. The world was certainly a peculiar place.

"What?" Violet said.

"Nothing." Erin crossed her arms. Violet looked at her expectantly, and Erin sighed. "I just don't understand the whole influencer thing. Like, who decided their opinion held more importance than anyone else's?"

Violet eyed her. "Oh, I get it."

"What?"

"You obviously haven't spent much time on social media."

Violet was right. Erin had spent pretty much zero time on

social media. She preferred traditional communication mediums, like phone calls instead of text messages and hand-written letters instead of email. Although she had embraced the speed, convenience, and necessity of email. But if she wanted to know what was going on in someone's life, she picked up the phone and called them instead of lurking behind a screen, giving various posts a thumbs-up to show she cared. And honestly, not being on social media certainly made it easier for her to grieve Adam's loss in private. There was something to be said about anonymity in a world of digital voyeurism.

Erin shrugged. "I don't see the big deal. What, suddenly because you have a camera attached to you at all times, you're a professional photographer? You know, just because I like to read doesn't make me a book critic."

Violet shook her head. "Not just anyone can do what he does." She pulled her phone from her pocket and brought up one of Nathan's social media profiles. She held it so Erin could see his posts, scrolling through photo after photo of places and dishes from around the world. Not all of the photos were shirtless, but the ones that were certainly demanded attention. But it was more than a half-naked man that made his posts special. He had an eye for capturing the natural beauty of his surroundings, including the colors and flavors of the food he'd eaten. "See? There's an art form to it."

"I guess so." If Erin wasn't careful, Nathan might make her a social media believer.

Violet rolled her eyes as she slid her phone back in her pocket. "Okay, I think I'm finished. Although I might check in on our new guest."

"Violet, leave Mr. Scott alone." Erin feigned admonishment before smiling.

Violet shrugged. "He might need extra towels or something."

"Oh, get outta here." Erin playfully patted Violet's shoulder as they both laughed and said their goodbyes.

The Abernathys shuffled toward the door, arm-in-arm. Mr. Abernathy tipped his hat toward Erin. "Don't wait up."

"I expect you to have her home at a reasonable hour," Erin teased.

"Don't count on it."

Erin laughed. "Have fun, you two."

She went to the dining room and cleared the dishes, scrubbing bits of food away before placing them in the dishwasher. She grabbed the soap, turned on the cycle, and sat at the table to catch her breath. She reached for a newspaper, soaking in the local gossip over her remaining cold cup of coffee with the low hum of the dishwasher to keep her company.

Erin's thoughts quickly drifted back to her new guest. If she didn't know better, she'd think he saw a ghost when he checked in. Maybe he wasn't the only one. It still struck her as odd when he slipped and said his name was Adam. And for someone who'd spent so much time in the public eye, he certainly acted strange. But then again, anything could be staged for a photograph.

Speaking of pictures, she certainly wasn't photo ready. She noticed a stain that appeared to be maple syrup on her shirt and felt too many stray hairs had left her ponytail. She desperately needed a shower. After downing the rest of her cold coffee, Erin folded the paper and left it on the table to go get cleaned up.

NATHAN'S HEART pounded in his chest as he slammed the door behind him. He opened and shut his eyes, squinting as he questioned his double vision. His mind had to be playing tricks on him. How was it possible he'd dreamt of this woman before meeting her? His imagination was often good, but there was no way it was *that* good. Was this what deja vu felt like?

And why in the world had he told her his name was Adam? None of it made any sense. He knew better than to blame it on jet lag.

Nathan remembered something he'd heard from an aboriginal during one of his visits to Australia. He'd met a woman named Alinta at an annual festival celebrating aboriginal culture. She'd told him he needed to cleanse his aura during a ceremonial burn. He'd looked at her with skepticism, but she had insisted he needed to let go of his past pain to find true happiness. She'd held out her hand and pulled him into a crowd surrounded by smoke. Swept up in the music and ceremonial dancing, he'd wondered if she cast a spell on him of some sort, since shortly after that, he'd experienced his first dream encounter with the blonde woman.

His host.

Not allowing his mind to wander any deeper, he distracted himself by getting settled into his temporary home. The room was cozy, with a king-size sleigh bed in the center of the room and a matching chest of drawers against the opposite wall. Floral and striped wallpaper adorned the walls, and a gold-framed mirror hung above a rolltop desk. The curtains were pulled back, the window revealing a clear view of the lush garden and courtyard below. He admired the warmth and European opulence as he unpacked a few things from his suitcase, hanging his nice clothes in the small closet.

Nathan pulled a laptop from his backpack and sat at the rolltop desk to check his email. He reviewed the TravelCon schedule and planned to drive over there on Thursday afternoon to check in and attend the first networking event. He'd received an email from Coco Bernstein letting him know the meeting with the television execs was scheduled for Saturday night at Osso Steakhouse. He knew Coco through Aunt Frances, although he hadn't actually met her yet. She'd been in public relations for over thirty years but had never represented a blogger before. Now that he was completely healed from his surgery and back on the road, it was time to consider what the next big career move would be. Television seemed like a logical jump, and it was something he'd always had in the back of his mind as a potential next step. After all, there were only so many sponsorship deals with travel companies and merchandise he wanted to continue doing.

As if on cue, his phone rang. It was Coco. "Darling, I'm not sure if you saw your email yet or not—"

"I'm looking at it as we speak," he said. Coco always followed up every email with a call.

"Great. You know how I am. I'm high touch, baby. You can't always rely on computers." She coughed, a thick smoker's cough to match her deep raspy voice. "Anywho, you're meeting with Jeff Fisher and Simon Wallace on Saturday evening to discuss a pilot idea they have. And dress sharp. Wear a nice suit or something. Don't show up in some hipster pair of jeans and a ratty T-shirt. Frances told me how you roll."

"Okay, noted." His lips curled up in a smile.

"And listen—I don't know how else to say it other than to come out with it, but you need to get a girlfriend."

Nathan laughed nervously. "What? Why?"

"From looking at some of your previous press, I've never seen you appear with a woman. Maybe you prefer the company of men, and that's okay too."

"I'm not—"

"Look, kid, you're being considered for television. And

take it from me, networks like to see stability in their assets, which is what you'd be to them. More than before, your behavior will be scrutinized, and not all press is good press. Understand?" She exhaled loudly, likely smoking a cigarette.

"Yeah, but how am I supposed to pull a girlfriend out of thin air on short notice?"

"You're a good-looking guy. I'm sure you have no problem charming the ladies. At a minimum, it might be nice for you to bring a date. A woman, you know? Or a man, whatever."

"I'm not gay."

"Hey, no judgment, okay? But it's hard to tell anything about you when you're flying solo to all your public appearances."

Nathan considered Coco's point. He'd never allowed himself to get serious with anyone and didn't want to muddy the waters between his personal and professional lives. Besides, most of his global trysts were short-lived and he liked it that way. No strings, no chance of it turning serious, and better yet, no chance of getting hurt. Yes, he may have unintentionally broken hearts in many ports throughout the world, but the one heart that was always spared was his. Just the way he liked it.

"This would really make me more viable to the network?"

"It couldn't hurt. Besides, Jeff and Simon will definitely bring their wives to dinner, so it might be nice if you had some arm candy of your own to round out the evening instead of being an awkward fifth wheel."

Coco certainly was old school, through and through. Nathan sighed. "Okay, I'll see what I can do."

"Great. Thanks, kiddo." She hung up.

Nathan stared at the lifeless phone screen after it faded to black. It wasn't enough pressure to turn on the charm for the network executives, but now he needed to charm a woman into being his date for the most important dinner of his career. Not that he lacked confidence in charming women, but he wanted to keep his eye on the prize for this weekend. He didn't need the complication or distraction of wooing someone, even temporarily. And the last thing he wanted was to act under false pretenses, so what kind of woman would agree to be his date-for-hire? At times like this, he could totally relate to that movie where the business-man hires a hooker to be at his beck and call. Not that he'd resort to that, and he doubted he'd be able to find a lady of the night in such a provincial place like Mystic Beach anyway. There had to be another way.

First things first. He'd promised the mayor he would spotlight the town on his blog and social media profiles. Perhaps during his exploration, he'd find a viable date for dinner Saturday night. His professional life depended on it, apparently.

Before he could think about it further, a scream inter-rupted his thoughts. His heart pounded as he rushed toward the cry for help.

4

$\mathcal{N}$athan ran downstairs toward the commotion, taking two steps at a time. The scream sounded serious, and he feared the worst as he finally made his way to the kitchen. Standing in the doorway, he heard expletives as the strong scent of detergent tickled his nose. A few bubbles floated toward him, landing on his shoulder as he panted heavily. He assessed the crisis that caused his host to scream.

His host was on her hands and knees, moving towels across the wood floors as she tried to dry up the abundance of water and soap overflowing from the dishwasher. Her towels were completely soaked; she was having about as much luck as if she were trying to manipulate wet concrete. He could hear her muttering words to herself, grunting as she tried helplessly to clean up the mess, but mostly, she was pushing water around.

"Woah, let's turn that thing off," he said. He gingerly stepped toward the dishwasher, careful not to let the sudsy tide take him down too. He fiddled with the controls, finally pushing the right button. The spinner inside the dishwasher slowly came to a stop, the last of the suds oozing from the sides. "That should help."

"Thanks," she said, continuing to glide across the soapy floor.

"Here, let me." He grabbed a towel and got down on his hands and knees to help her clean up soapocalypse.

She didn't argue, pushing a rogue strand of hair out of her face. Sweat glinted off her forehead as she gathered the soaked towels and carefully took them into the nearby laundry room. She returned with fresh towels and threw a couple in his direction as she quickly dropped to clean up more soap. She shook her head. "I can't believe I did that."

"Mistakes happen," he said, swapping out wet towels for dry ones. He pushed them in big sweeping motions across the floor to catch the last remnants of water and soap.

"Yeah, a possibly expensive one at that." She sighed and shook her head as she looked at the walnut floors. "How much damage do you think?" She bit her bottom lip, cringing in anticipation of hearing the worst.

He paused, his attention drawn to her mouth. He wondered how her bottom lip tasted, how he longed to find out. Realizing he was staring, he assessed their surroundings. It was easy to see most of the wood was salvageable if they moved quickly to properly dry it out. Likely, what took the biggest blow was her ego.

He felt the stress radiating off her and couldn't help assessing her too. Even in these circumstances, she was beautiful. Her forehead wrinkled with stress, her lips pursed, and bumpy ridges popped out on top of her blonde ponytail. Her shirt was damp from lugging wet towels into the laundry room, and he tried so hard not to stare as he admired her curves. He imagined peeling her out of those wet layers, discovering every inch of her smooth skin.

His mind must have wandered a little too far, since her

eyes widened as she looked back at him, waiting for his response. He cleared his throat. "Hard to say, but it looks like most of this could be salvaged."

Erin's shoulders relaxed. "I hope you're right."

"I'm seldom wrong." His lips turned up slightly.

Erin smiled. "Oh, *really*? Would Mrs. Scott agree?"

"No Mrs. to speak of," he said, holding her gaze. She looked away, and if he didn't know any better, he'd say her cheeks turn pink. "And shouldn't your husband be here to rescue you from faulty dishwashers?"

"Operator."

"Your husband is an operator?"

"No—faulty dishwasher *operator*." She pointed at her chest. "And no husband." She looked away, a ripple of pain visible across her face. "He died," she volunteered, picking at something invisible on her mostly see-through shirt.

"Wow, I'm so sorry." *Way to go, moron.* "How long ago?" He couldn't help prying. He wanted to know more about this woman, barely resisting the urge to pull her close and brush his fingers through her coconut-scented hair. But his inquiring mind also didn't excuse him from being nosey. "If you don't mind my asking."

"It's okay," she assured. "About a year. A freak motorcycle accident. Fortunately, he didn't suffer, at least that's what the medical staff told me."

"Well, that's good." He didn't know what else to say. He could see ribbons of pain behind her strong facade and couldn't imagine how Erin must have felt losing her husband. He wished he could take it all away, fighting the urge to take her into his arms and hold her, allowing her to let it all go.

And it was that very reason he never allowed himself to get too involved with someone. He couldn't imagine rebounding from a loss that tremendous. It had been hard

37

enough when his mom walked out, and she might even still be alive. Even when his father died, he didn't talk much for about a month, and nothing Frances did was enough to bring him out of his funk. He still felt partially responsible for his father's death, which weighed heavily on his conscience if he allowed it. So, as he glanced at his soap-covered companion, he couldn't help feeling fortunate for never having loved someone so much that his world stopped when it was over. Someone doesn't just rebound from an experience like that, no matter how tough they might be.

"Why no Mrs. for you?" she asked, looking at him from under her eyelashes.

Nathan shrugged. "Occupational hazard, I guess. I'm rarely in the same place for long."

"Oh, right." She paused. "And in all your travels, you never made it to Mystic Beach? What took you so long?" The corners of her lips turned up as she teased him.

"I guess I needed an invitation," he joked. "I'm not usually a small town kinda guy, but now that I'm here, I'm kicking myself for not getting here sooner." He locked onto her green eyes, and the air sparked with electricity.

Erin blushed as she looked back at the floors, breaking the spell. "I guess I better call a flooring expert." She rubbed her forehead and groaned. "I really don't need the unexpected expense right now." Her eyes grew wide, realizing she'd overshared.

Instinctively, Nathan touched her shoulder. An electric current coursed through his veins as his hand made contact with her delicate skin. "Don't worry, it doesn't suit you." *Where did that come from?* He'd never said those words in his entire life. Erin studied him, just as surprised at his words. "Sorry." His brow furrowed as he broke the connection, awkwardly bringing his hand back to his side before getting up. "Well, I better get going. Are you going to be okay?"

Erin paused. "Yeah, I'm fine. I'm sure you're busy." She waved her hands. He thought he saw disappointment in her eyes. Before he could contradict her, she said, "Thanks again for your help. If it weren't for you, I probably would have drowned in soap by now."

He smiled. "I doubt that, but I'm glad I could save you." He stood there, unsure of what to say, but for some reason, his feet felt cemented to the floor.

"Okay, I guess I better wash these towels," she said. He held out his hand to help her stand, and their electrical current charged the room. "Have a good day, Mr. Scott, and thanks again."

"Yes, you too Ms. …?"

"Erin. My name is Erin."

"Nice to meet you."

"We've already met." She smiled.

"Oh, right. Okay, I'm leaving now." What had gotten into him?

"Bye." She giggled.

He walked toward the doorway and paused. "You can call me Nathan, by the way."

"Okay, Nathan." His name on her lips had never sounded so good. He turned again to say something, anything. *Dude, walk away*. Reluctantly, he did.

ERIN PUT the last of the damp towels in the washing machine, double checking to ensure she used the correct type of soap before leaving it to run its cycle. She couldn't get Nathan's words out of her mind: *Don't worry, it doesn't suit you*. That's something Adam would say to her, and her skin broke out in goose pimples hearing the phrase again. Sometimes she couldn't help feeling like he was still with her, and this certainly solidified it in her mind.

After Adam died, she went to a few psychic medium live events, hoping he'd come through with something to say to comfort her. He always had the right words, and she longed to have one more conversation with him, even if it wasn't his body standing in front of her. She swore she'd know it was an authentic experience with a medium because of Adam's unique way of expressing himself that could only be summed up as *Adam*. Hearing his words again, albeit through a different man's mouth, comforted her somehow.

And Nathan certainly was different.

She smiled as she recounted his awkward behavior in the kitchen. If she didn't know better, it seemed like he was grasping at excuses not to leave. For someone in the public eye on a regular basis, he certainly behaved oddly, but some-how, it struck her as endearing. She could definitely under-stand why Nathan had the following he did. There was something special about him. Magnetic, perhaps. And yes, he was certainly easy on the eyes.

It surprised Erin to hear he was single, although she could understand that being an occupational hazard. She couldn't imagine dating someone who traveled across the world and hardly spent any time at home, let alone someone who spent a lot of time in the spotlight. A self-proclaimed homebody, she didn't even make it to Boston to visit her father and his new wife but maybe once every two or three years. And she'd never made it to visit her brother, Kyle, in the handful of ports the Navy had stationed him. There was no way she could travel on a regular basis, which would be the only way a relationship with someone like Nathan could work.

Why was she musing about a relationship with Nathan?

Shaking her head, she assessed the kitchen to see what additional cleaning she needed to do to get things back to normal. She wiped the inside of the dishwasher to ensure all the soapy residue was gone to avoid another mishap, staving off the inevitable call to her insurance adjuster just a little longer.

Calling Ted Bailey was never high on her list. She avoided him at all costs and wished he didn't have the best insurance rates in town. Sometimes, she weighed whether the cost of doing business with creepy Ted was really worth it to save a couple hundred on her policy on an annual basis, but she wasn't currently in a position to be choosy.

Ripping off the proverbial Band-Aid, Erin tried his office a few times and got voicemail. She'd likely need to visit him in person, and she secretly wondered if Ted were dodging her calls, hoping it would force her into an office visit. What excuse could she use if he asked her out again? She shuddered at the thought.

Hoping Ted would return her call and she could avoid seeing him in person, Erin put on a kettle for tea and sat at the kitchen table to catch her breath while the water roared to life. She flipped through the paper she'd started reading that morning, unable to concentrate on the words. The room still carried a charge from the sparks between her and Nathan. But she wasn't ready to consider a relationship with anyone, was she? Adam had died only thirteen months ago. He perfectly embodied everything she'd ever wanted in a husband and a best friend. She counted herself extremely lucky to have felt true love once in her life and felt skeptical it could happen again. Besides, she had her hands full with the inn and was determined to make the best of it. She owed it to Aunt Nancy, who had entrusted Erin with her life's work. She didn't want to let it all go up in smoke and let her family down.

"Knock, knock," Brooke said, entering through the back door off the kitchen. Brooke Santos, Erin's friend since high school, had stayed in Mystic Beach and opened a bakery in town with the help of her family. Since Erin didn't have the patience to bake, Brooke had agreed to supply her with sweet treats for her guests.

"Perfect timing. I just put a kettle on for tea." She stood to take the bags from Brooke's arms, giving her a hug after she'd set them on the table. "It's good to see you."

Brooke studied Erin with her hazel eyes. "You've had a rough day."

"Is it that obvious?" Erin's brow wrinkled.

"It's okay. I brought you something that should help." Brooke unpacked the bags, pulling out coffee cakes, breakfast breads, and cookies, putting some in the fridge and freezer. She left a small bag with cookies on the table. "These will be perfect with our tea." Brooke paused, assessing the kitchen. "What happened here?"

As if on cue, the kettle whistled, and Erin got to work fixing their tea. "You won't believe the day I've had."

Brooke pushed a dark curly strand behind her ear as she took a seat at the table. "Go on."

Erin sighed. "Somehow, I mixed up the dish detergent with dishwasher liquid and created a big, wet, soapy mess in here." She brought two mugs to the table.

"A lack of sleep makes you do strange things." Brooke somehow knew Erin had had a hard time sleeping in recent months. It had taken Erin a while to get used to not sharing the bed with Adam anymore, and she still used a body pillow to distract her mind from the emptiness.

"Believe it or not, I actually slept pretty well last night."

Brooke drizzled honey into her mug while she let her tea steep. "Is there something on your mind that's distracting you?"

Erin considered her friend's question. She couldn't come out and say how dire her financial situation was with the inn.

Instead, she decided to broach it in an indirect way. "I guess I've been a little preoccupied with figuring out how to increase occupancy."

Brooke slid the cookies out of their bag onto a nearby plate. "Isn't that blogger supposed to stay here?"

Erin paused. "How do you know about Nathan?"

Brooke smiled. "Have you forgotten how small this town is? Everyone talks." She removed her tea bag and sipped. "And it's Nathan, huh?" Her eyebrows raised.

"Yeah, he actually helped me with the soapy mishap in here."

"Word on the street is he's easy on the eyes."

Erin shrugged. "If you're into guys who are never home."

"And he's helpful. Sounds like a catch."

Erin blushed. "I guess."

"So, let me get this straight. You've got a hot travel blogger with a huge following staying here for free, and you're trying to figure out how to increase occupancy. Hmm…what's a girl to do?" Brooke held out her hands, pretending to weigh options.

"What are you saying?" Erin already knew but put on her best poker face anyway.

Brooke rolled her eyes. "Why don't you ask him to post about your inn to his thousands of blog followers? That should help with one of your problems."

"But he's staying here as a favor to the mayor," Erin objected. "I'm not sure I can ask that of him." She wasn't sure how the whole influencer thing worked. Maybe he had guidelines to follow from Marco.

"Why can't you? Besides, he was quick to help you clean up a mess earlier. Why would he say no to helping you with something much less messy?"

Erin drummed her fingers against her mug as she considered Brooke's words. Nathan was spotlighting Mystic Beach as a whole. Even if Marco gave him guidelines, why couldn't she ask that her inn be a part of it as well? "You have a point."

Brooke slid the plate of cookies in front of Erin. "Here, have a cookie. It will give you courage."

Erin wasn't sure how, but Brooke's baked goods often evoked some kind of emotion when she ate them. Her blueberry breakfast bread tasted like happiness, often leaving Erin feeling completely carefree. Brooke even managed to make cookies around Valentine's Day that tasted like a first kiss. Erin studied the cookies, which on the surface appeared to be a gingersnap. "For real?"

"Somehow, I knew you needed a boost today. Go on." Brooke nodded her head. "Take a bite."

Erin brought the cookie to her lips, letting it crumble over her tongue. The ginger and cardamom flavors tickled her palate. As she ate the second bite, she felt more invigorated. She looked at the kitchen floor. "I guess I need to call a handyman. Do you know of anyone?"

Brooke nodded. "Yeah, I'll give you a number to call. But shouldn't you call Ted Bailey first?"

Erin cringed. "Yeah, I left him a voicemail already."

"You know you'll likely have to go visit him in person."

"That's what I feared." Ted Bailey refused to take no for an answer, which probably made him really good at what he did. But when it came to his advances, he'd chalked Erin's disinterest up to widow's grief, stressing that he'd be ready to take her out when she felt up to it. What he never seemed to understand was she'd never be interested in him for anything other than a good rate on her policy.

"Aren't you forgetting something else?" Brooke looked at her expectantly.

"I'll talk to him when he gets back," Erin mumbled through another bite of her courage cookie. "And thanks." She appreciated Brooke helping her establish new patterns of normalcy since Adam had died, pushing her to practice self-care through better sleep and taking time for herself. She felt grateful for having someone like Brooke welcome her home to Mystic Beach with open arms, helping her piece her life back together after things fell apart.

"That's what I'm here for, girl," Brooke said. "After all, what's the worst that could happen?"

Erin thought about Nathan. How quickly he'd come to her rescue earlier in the kitchen, his endearingly awkward goodbye, and how his eyes pierced right through to her soul. She couldn't quite put her finger on it, but something was different, yet familiar, about him. Maybe whatever was in the courage cookie would help her figure that out too.

5

*C*ould he have been any more awkward?

Nathan walked through downtown Mystic Beach with his digital camera in hand, ready to capture the essence of what made the coastal town special. His mind wasn't helping with his need to focus, replaying how he'd reintroduced himself and gawked at Erin in her damp T-shirt. It was almost like he'd regressed to his teenage years again, blown away whenever a pretty girl acknowledged his existence. Even covered in soap and completely frazzled, there was no denying Erin was a total babe.

Was it just him, or did she seem interested in him too? Those sparks he felt couldn't have been one-sided. He considered himself pretty in-tune with his surroundings, including people's body language. He could easily pick up on signals when they were thrown his way, and all signs pointed to go. He imagined what would have happened if he'd stayed even five minutes longer. He probably would have found out exactly what her bottom lip tasted like. He shook away the thought, reminding himself she'd just lost her husband a little over a year ago. Besides, he needed to stay focused. He had a job to do for the mayor while he was in town.

Storefronts and restaurants lined the appropriately named Main Street, with modern and Spanish influences easily seen in the town's architecture. He passed The Blue Cask, resisting the temptation to go in for a charcuterie board and chardonnay. The smell of freshly baked sourdough bread emitting from The Mystic Vine didn't help either as he watched a waiter fan white tablecloths across bistro tables in preparation for hungry patrons to sit on the front patio and watch the town go by.

A family pushing a stroller passed by on his left, and three bicyclists rolled down the main drag looking for a place to park for lunch. Mystic Beach was enveloped by a redwood preserve to the north and the coast to the west, the waves crashing against the shore in the distance temporarily hypnotizing Nathan.

He raised his camera to his eye, capturing the natural beauty around him. Searching for the perfect light to line up a shot, he stopped in his tracks when Erin strolled through his line of vision. She looked determined as she crossed the street, obviously with a destination in mind. He followed her with his camera as a tall, lanky male grabbed her elbow, stopping her in her tracks. No boyfriend, huh?

Nathan's heart sank a little as he forced himself to focus his lens elsewhere. He took a few shots of buildings with mountains in the background, examining his quick work through the camera's preview screen. But curiosity got the best of him, and his attention drifted back toward Erin. He ignored the thoughts of being a peeping Tom as he focused his lens on her. She crossed her arms, her facial expression appearing tense. Did his eyes deceive him, or did she seem uncomfortable around this guy?

His grip tightened on the camera. Something felt off.

Maybe he should cross the street and do a casual run-in, just to be sure she was okay.

❀

ERIN FOCUSED on putting one foot in front of the other, ignoring her body's desire to run in the opposite direction. Dread washed over her as she prepared herself for a conversation with Ted Bailey. If she ever wished a time machine had been invented, it was now. She'd go back in time and tell her aunt to work with anyone but Ted, despite his promise of the lowest rates in town. Someone, anyone, had to offer better rates when the creep factor was taken into account. Did she have a congresswoman she could write about advocating for a creepy guy tariff or tax? She cracked a smile at the thought.

When she approached his office, a sign on the door indicated he was out to lunch and would be back shortly. Part of her was relieved she wouldn't have to see Ted, but another part felt annoyed for drawing this out any longer than necessary. She searched her purse for a pen and paper to leave a note to have him call her. As she scribbled on a random receipt, someone tugged on her elbow, making her pen go off the page in a straight line.

"You lookin' for me?" Ted smiled.

She took a deep breath. *Okay, let's keep this as brief as possible.* "Yes, as a matter of fact, I am. I need your help."

"Ah, so you need me, huh?" He ogled her.

Erin's skin crawled as she folded her arms over her chest. "Yeah, I guess. My dishwasher malfunctioned this morning, and it left quite a mess in my kitchen. I think I need to file a claim against my policy."

He shook his head, tongue clicking against his teeth.

"What a shame. I can imagine things must have gotten pretty…wet, huh?"

Erin held back the desire to vomit, taking a barely noticeable step back. "I guess."

"I suppose I need to come out and assess the damage myself as part of the claim," he said. "And we probably should talk about increasing your coverage to one of our comprehensive bed and breakfast policies. How about this evening? We can discuss it all over dinner after my house call." He ran a knuckle down her arm in an attempt at seduction, which did nothing to quell Erin's upchuck reflex.

"Sorry I'm late," Nathan said, approaching Erin's side.

Ted took a step back and sneered. "I'm sorry, who are you?"

"I'm Nathan," he said, stepping protectively in front of Erin before holding out a hand to shake. "And you are?"

Ted crossed his arms, refusing Nathan's friendly gesture. "I'm her insurance agent." He looked at Erin. "You didn't tell me you had a…*boyfriend*." He said the word with total disdain, like it left a bitter taste on his tongue. Perhaps Erin wasn't the only one trying to keep upchuck reflexes at bay.

Out of the corner of her eye, Erin saw Ted's office manager, Valerie Prescott, stop dead in her tracks. One of the biggest town gossips, she was obviously coming back from lunch. Her eyes lit up; she must have heard what Ted said. Valerie quickly averted her gaze and made quick work with the front door lock, practically trotting back to her desk to stir up trouble.

Oh, dear God.

Before Erin could correct him, Nathan continued, "I'm glad you two had a chance to catch up. She's been so worried after the mess in the kitchen this morning." Nathan reached over and massaged Erin's shoulders. "How you holding up?"

Erin caught her jaw before it completely fell to the

ground. Shockwaves pulsated through her body from his strong touch, making her knees buckle. "Better, thanks," she finally managed to squeak out.

Ted scowled, straightening his stance. "Well, I suggest you call Hank Vargas today to help with the clean-up and to ensure no further damage is done. Just keep your receipts and we'll reimburse. I can squeeze in some time tomorrow afternoon to do an assessment for the claim. Will that be—"

"That'd be great," Nathan cut him off. "We'll both be there." He wrapped an arm around Erin, who could only nod in agreement.

Ted, visibly annoyed, confirmed the appointment time and quickly said goodbye before escaping into his office, leaving Erin and Nathan on the street together.

"You didn't have to do that," Erin said.

"That guy seemed like a total creep."

"You have no idea." She shook her head. "He's been trying to get me to go out with him since high school but can't take a hint. And now that I've moved back, I guess he thinks he's got a chance."

"I'm glad I could help." Nathan smiled.

Erin peered through the glass front of Ted's office, watching Valerie flex her jaw at a mile a minute on the phone. "Of all times for her to show up too."

"Who is she?"

"Oh, just one of the town gossips. Now, everyone is going to think you're my boyfriend." She averted her gaze, trying her best to ignore the swarm of nerves fluttering around in her stomach.

Nathan shrugged. "Better than everyone thinking *he* is." He nodded toward Ted's office.

Erin chuckled. "You really don't mind being there tomorrow when he shows up to assess the damage?"

"Of course not. That's what boyfriends are for, right?" He winked.

Erin blushed, feeling a wave of desire course through her body from his playful wink. She looked at Nathan, channeling what was left of her courage cookie. "So, since you're my 'boyfriend' and you're 'internet famous,' I was wondering if you wouldn't mind giving the inn some publicity. You know, share a few photos, or write a blog post, or whatever it is you do." She used air quotes around internet famous. And boyfriend.

Nathan held back a smile. "Whatever it is I do, huh?" He folded his arms and leaned against a light post.

"Yeah, I'm not going to pretend to understand it," she said. When Nathan didn't respond right away, her confidence wavered. "I mean, if that's not too much to ask."

"No, I'd be happy to," he said. "Your inn is very charming."

"Thanks." She smiled. They kept their eyes locked on one another, unsure of what to say next but not ready to walk away.

"What's good to eat around here?" Nathan asked.

Erin looked around Main Street. "Well, The Chowder House has the best lobster rolls if you're in the mood for something like that."

Nathan feigned skepticism. "I don't know, I've had some really good lobster rolls in my day."

"These will change your mind," she challenged.

"We'll see about that." Nathan paused. "Will you join me?" He held out his elbow for her to grab.

Erin placed her hand through the crook of his arm, feeling his muscles flex under her fingertips. "Yes, but only because I want to see the look on your face when you see that I'm right."

Nathan smiled. "See? You're totally acting like my girlfriend after all. Already telling me I'm wrong."

Erin laughed. "Get used to it."

Nathan laughed. "I bet I could."

His words surprised Erin, making her heart flutter. Parts of her stirred back to life. Parts she'd feared had atrophied when Adam died. She took a deep breath, feeling happy at the prospect of her heart glowing once again, even if it were just a ruse to keep creepy Ted off her back for a week. She'd appreciate it for what it was, for however long it lasted.

I BET I COULD.

Nathan's own words echoed in his mind, and he realized how true they felt. He stole a glance at Erin, the woman he'd just made his fake girlfriend in a knee-jerk reaction to ward off a creep, as they walked toward The Chowder House. He'd never been in a real relationship, let alone a fake one. With his second chance at life, he'd certainly gotten used to experiencing more firsts, but Erin was totally unexpected.

He didn't blame Ted for trying; she certainly seemed like a catch. She was beautiful and smart and had a good sense of humor. She even looked adorable when she was stressed out, and there was no way he could ever forget how her wet T-shirt hugged her curves after the disaster in the kitchen that morning. What wasn't to like about the woman?

Erin pointed to a bakery, drawing Nathan's attention back to the present. "Better save room for dessert. Batter Up Bakery is the best."

Nathan patted his stomach. "We'll see. I'm not normally a sweets person."

"Yeah, but Brooke's sweets are different. They're an experience."

"Experience?"

"Yeah, and she's my best friend, so…"

"I've never heard of anything from a bakery being considered an experience."

"That's because you haven't been there yet."

Nathan chuckled. "Okay, you win. I'll save room."

"Good."

They approached The Chowder House, and Nathan held open the door for Erin. With the weather being cooperative, they agreed to sit outside on the patio. The host led them toward a table with a yellow umbrella blocking the sun and a clear view of Mystic Beach. A light breeze helped carry the sails on a sailboat on the horizon, and Nathan watched a couple of fishermen throw lines in the water at a nearby pier, hoping to bring home a brag-worthy catch.

"Great view," Nathan said, admiring the picturesque scene, including his companion.

Erin nodded. "I didn't realize how special it was until I came back. It's nice and clear today."

"What brought you back?"

"My aunt Nancy. I took over the inn for her when she died."

Nathan set down his menu. "Wow, I'm so sorry."

Erin shook her head. "It's okay. It's weird because it's not like we were super close, at least in recent years. I can't help feeling she left it to me by default since my mother died, and there aren't any other living relatives on that side of my family."

"What happened to your mom?"

"Breast cancer." She recounted when she got that call. Stage four with a weak prognosis and limited treatment options. Her mother encouraged her to take a genetic test to see if she was susceptible. Erin was going to blow it off, but her brother insisted. Thankfully, the test came back negative, but she lost her mom three months later.

Nathan shook his head. "Wow."

Erin paused. "Oh gosh, I must sound depressing. Dead mother, dead aunt, dead husband." She laughed nervously. "I assure you I do have living relatives. My dad lives in Boston with his new wife, and my brother, Kyle, is on active duty in the Navy. I think the last post card he sent me was from Guam."

"Guam. Lovely place." Nathan cringed slightly.

"You've been?"

He nodded. "Yeah. I actually got stuck there for forty-eight hours when a plane's engine failed. Can't say I'm in a huge hurry to go back."

Erin shook her head. "I don't see how you do it."

"What?"

"Travel. For a living. Don't you get tired of living out of your suitcase?"

Nathan smiled. "You sound like my aunt Frances."

"She's a smart woman."

"You have no idea."

Their waiter arrived to take their order, both of them settling on unsweetened iced tea and lobster rolls.

"So, where is Frances?" Erin asked.

"Seattle. That's home base for me, whenever I *do* unpack my suitcase."

"Never been up there. I don't travel much," she admitted.

"It's a great place."

"If you like gray weather, right?"

He smiled. "Yeah, it's pretty gray there. But it accentuates the beauty of the tall, lush trees, making everything appear more alive."

She grinned. "I can see how you're good at what you do."

"Oh, yeah? How so?" He raised an eyebrow.

"You just sold me on the beauty of Seattle, when isn't that also the city with the highest suicide rate?"

"Seasonal affective disorder is a real thing," he conceded. "Why do you think I travel so much?"

Erin smiled. "You know, you could move your home base to somewhere sunnier. That *is* an option."

Nathan shook his head. "I couldn't leave Frances behind. Permanently anyway. I owe my life to her."

"How do you mean?"

"She raised me." Raising him was a severe understatement. She'd saved him. If it weren't for her, he wasn't sure where he would have ended up, considering both his parents gave up on him. Gave up on themselves.

"What happened to your parents?" she asked.

Nathan paused, realizing he was on the brink of oversharing. He normally kept things very light in conversation with women—or anyone else for that matter. He wasn't prepared to bare his heart to an almost-stranger, despite how at-ease he felt being around her.

"Nathan?" The voice interrupted his thoughts. He and Erin looked toward their greeter, watching Marco and Elise walk toward them.

Nathan stood. "Hey, Marco." As the mayor approached, Nathan held out his hand to shake. Marco's grip was strong and sturdy.

"You've come to one of the best spots in town, with an excellent tour guide, I see." Marco rocked back and forth on the balls of his feet as he made eye contact with Erin.

"Yes, Erin has been an absolute gem," Nathan said, smiling at her. "And speaking of gems, you've got a charming little town here. I hope to make you proud with the feature."

"I have no doubt you will," Marco said. "Did you order lobster rolls?"

"Of course. They're the best," Erin said.

"Have you two eaten?" Nathan asked. "You're welcome to join us if you'd like."

"No, that's—" Elise started.

"Yes, that would—" Marco said. They both giggled, looking at one another before Elise conceded and they joined the table.

"I'm still skeptical these lobster rolls are the best," Nathan said. "They've got some fierce competition. My all-time favorite is from—"

"Dock and Roll in Maine. I remember seeing the photo you shared," Elise mused, supporting her chin in a palm as she leaned toward Nathan.

Their waiter came to the table and quickly amended their order to include Marco and Elise.

"The owner here is from Maine originally," Marco offered. "And don't mind my bride-to-be. She has a crush on you." Marco winced, and Nathan heard some shuffling under the table. "Good thing I'm a confident man." Marco reached over to hold Elise's hand, who smiled at him through gritted teeth. Marco leaned over and kissed her cheek, and her embarrassment melted away. "Sorry for embarrassing you, sweetheart."

"I think a trip to Batter Up will fix things," Elise said.

"We'll see," Marco said, patting his stomach. "I'm trying to maintain my girlish figure for our big day."

"Well, if you want me to continue convincing Vince Paluzzo to be our Travel Ambassador, you'll take me there," Elise quipped.

"Okay, you win." Marco chuckled, holding up his hands in defeat. "Can you at least allow me to keep my dignity in front of our company?" He nodded toward Nathan and Erin.

Elise pretended to maintain her tough facade, but one look from Marco quickly melted it away. She smiled and agreed.

"You two seem really happy," Erin said.

"We are." Elise held Marco's hand. "We try to keep business as separate as possible, which helps."

"Elise and I are on the city council together," Marco offered to Nathan. "It was actually her idea to ask you to visit our town and do a feature."

"I'm glad she did," Nathan said, smiling at the happy couple. He stole a glance at Erin, who met his gaze before quickly looking away.

Their waiter brought their dishes, and Nathan eyed his lobster roll before taking a picture. "Occupational hazard," he shrugged.

"Of course," Marco mumbled through a bite.

"So, Nathan, are you single?" Elise asked as she grabbed the pepper shaker.

Marco slightly choked on his sandwich. "Elise, don't pry."

"What?" Elise looked at both Nathan and Erin, a proverbial light bulb going off above her head. "Oh, I see." She pointed to Erin and then Nathan. "You two, am I right? I can see the chemistry."

Nathan and Erin exchanged a look, neither one knowing what to say.

"And here we just crashed your lunch date." Elise tsked. "I'm so sorry. We'll eat and run."

"It's no problem," Nathan said. "Don't rush." He was in no hurry to return to where he and Erin left off in their conversation. He preferred to keep things light and avoid discussing his past.

"Yeah, it's totally fine," Erin reassured their guests. She sounded a little less convincing than Nathan, but that could have been his imagination.

"Marco, you weren't kidding. This is legit." Nathan pointed at his lobster roll.

"Better than Dock and Roll's?" Marco raised an eyebrow.

Nathan paused. "Maybe." He grinned.

Elise clapped. "Can we use that in our marketing?"

"Elise, stop harassing the poor man." Marco waved his hands in her direction. She stuck out her tongue at Marco, and both of them giggled like teenagers.

Nathan took out his wallet and said he would treat everyone to lunch. Marco took out his credit card and insisted on picking up the bill instead. "Besides, we're the ones who crashed your lunch, and you're our guest," Marco insisted.

"Fine, you win," Nathan conceded. "And thanks, this is very kind."

"We talked about chamber business, didn't we?" Elise asked.

"What's the latest with that surfer?" Erin asked.

"Ah, see? Now we can definitely expense this." Marco smiled. "Our biggest scandal at the moment is a surfer who has chained himself to a lamp post down at the beach in an act to raise awareness for beach preservation." Marco rolled his eyes. "These kids, I swear."

"Have you figured out how to get him loose?" Erin asked.

Elise grimaced. "Afraid not. We are evaluating our budget to see if we have additional funds to put toward preserving our shoreline but nothing concrete yet."

"We'll figure it out," Marco said. "We always do." He smiled at Elise, whose cheeks turned a little pink. "Erin, you should show Nathan the Brannan Point lighthouse while you're both down here."

Before Erin could agree, Nathan shook his head. "Actually, I need to run. I have some things to take care of in preparation for my conference tomorrow evening." He looked at Erin, who appeared slightly disappointed. Small price to pay to avoid picking up where they left off before Marco and Elise crashed their date. Lunch. Whatever this was.

Erin nodded. "Yeah, that sounds good. I have stuff to take care of at the inn anyway."

Nathan's phone rang. *Saved by the bell.* "I need to take this. Thanks again for lunch. It was amazing." He stood and walked away to take his call. It was Coco.

"Just wanted to give you the heads up that your dinner meeting could possibly move to Friday instead. Simon might have a scheduling conflict, but they're trying to resolve it."

"Okay, thanks for the heads up."

"Any luck finding a date?"

Nathan's mind wandered to Erin. "Maybe."

"Well, get on it, kid. Time's ticking. Pay her if you have to." She hung up.

Nathan looked at the black screen on his phone. Coco certainly had a unique way of communicating, and he wasn't sure he'd ever get used to it. But Coco made it clear, despite her minimal words. He needed to show the executives he was stable in all aspects of his life. That he was a sure thing to bet on for their pilot.

He was so close to gaining everything he'd ever wanted. He thoroughly enjoyed the thrill of exploring new places, new faces, and capturing the essence of new experience with every snap of his camera and every taste of exotic dishes. He was in the best shape of his life, finally having a physical heart that could keep up with his figurative one. No one was better for this role than him, and he felt it in his bones. Now he just needed to secure a date for dinner.

Given the amount of time he'd be in town, Nathan also didn't need any more drama. His visit to Mystic Beach would come to a close in a matter of a few days, and he'd be off to who knows where in the world. He didn't have time to get invested in a relationship and wasn't interested in anything long-term. Despite what little he actually knew about her at that point, he got the sense that Erin was a no-drama kind of woman. She was the perfect woman to ask this favor. And he'd helped her out of a bind that morning with creepy Ted. Surely, she'd be up for returning a favor.

Nathan needed to keep it balanced, though. He couldn't quite put his finger on it, but something about her was different. He'd almost opened up to her at lunch and told her his life story. Something about her put him at ease, almost like she felt familiar to him somehow. Well, he'd only been dreaming about her for months, which still shocked the hell out of him.

He drew in a breath. The sooner he asked her, the better. And if luck would have it, maybe she'd be willing to help him move into the next phase of his career.

6

---

*E*rin pulled out of the Halbert's parking lot after picking up some provisions for the next few days. She thought running some errands would help distract her from overthinking about her relationship with Nathan. On one hand, she felt thankful for him saving her from a very uncomfortable situation with Ted. On the other, she knew word traveled fast in Mystic Beach, especially when Valerie got involved. Surely, Ted's receptionist would be dying to tell everyone about something as juicy as this.

Erin never enjoyed being in the spotlight, always keeping a low profile and doing her best to fly under the radar. And despite his best intentions, being mistaken for Nathan's girl-friend would put her front and center in the town's gossip mill. How would she handle it when people did what they normally do—talk?

She had two options. She could be honest about the misunderstanding. After all, it was insinuated from purely coincidental circumstances. She could also plead the fifth, telling people to mind their own business for once, which is what she really wanted to do. Of course, she knew that would only fuel the fire, giving people even more to talk about.

Besides, it wasn't like there was any shame in leveraging the situation to her advantage. He was an influencer, whatever that meant, and could help her spread the word about The Gilded Rose. It was a completely innocent exchange of services.

But if she were being completely honest, Nathan made her think less than innocent thoughts. She still felt heat where his hand had lingered on her skin during their interaction with Ted. She couldn't help imagining what it would be like to feel his touch on other areas of her body, sparking to life parts of her that had been dormant for so long. She hadn't felt that way since Adam first touched her, and Nathan's touch had a warmth, a familiarity about it that made absolutely no logical sense.

A part of her felt she was somehow betraying Adam, despite the lack of merit to her *relationship* with Nathan. She had finally adjusted to a sense of normalcy alone, slowly removing the scar tissue on her heart from losing Adam. She wasn't ready to endure any potential heartache. Not yet anyway. Her heart couldn't handle another painful loss. Although she was starting to question if she would ever be ready. Thankfully, she didn't need to know the answer to that right now. *One day at a time.*

Without realizing it, she'd parked outside of Batter Up. She wasn't getting anywhere thinking herself in circles. She needed to talk to Brooke. If all else failed, maybe Brooke had whipped up a clarity mousse, or a magic eight bread that Erin could consult for answers. Better yet, maybe she had a cloaking pudding to avoid town gossip.

She didn't bother going through the storefront like a normal patron, instead going around to the back of the building and entering through the kitchen. She knew that was where she'd find Brooke anyway. When she crossed the threshold, the smell of lemon and blueberry flooded her senses. There was something else too; warmth, swaying in a hammock with a good book, and sunshine warming her skin. She knew going there would make her feel better.

"Hey, girl." Brooke popped up from around a corner, smudges of flour acting as eye black under her eyes. "I'd hug you but..." She shrugged, looking down at her apron covered in unknown substances.

"I'll consider myself hugged." Erin smiled. "What smells so good?"

"It's a new recipe I'm trying for a lemon blueberry loaf. Unofficially, it's sunshine bread." A timer beeped and Brooke grabbed oven mitts, taking the sunshine bread out of the oven. She placed it on a trivet to cool. "So, when were you planning to tell me you and Nathan are a thing?" She playfully elbowed Erin.

Erin shook her head. "Gossips."

"I thought you were going to ask him for help with the inn. And then I hear from Betsy Jenkins you're in a relationship?" Brooke wiggled her brow. "*That* was fast."

Erin sighed. "It's a huge misunderstanding." When Brooke gave her a confused look, she continued. "Nathan came to my rescue with Ted Bailey, sparing me from his advances. Ted called Nathan my boyfriend and Valerie Prescott was there and heard everything. Neither one of us denied it since it helped Ted back off."

Brooke nodded. "Right place at the right time. Don't blame you for playing along since Ted was involved." She grimaced.

"Yeah, but somehow I knew this would cause more grief than it's worth."

"Wait, you *did* ask your new boyfriend to help with your

inn, right?" Brooke smiled, obviously having fun at Erin's expense.

"Yeah, and the cookies were a nice boost, by the way."

"Perks of dating an internet star," Brooke mused.

"It's not real." Erin playfully elbowed Brooke as they laughed. Then Erin's thoughts wandered back to Adam, and her heart ached. What would he think of all of this? She knew deep down he'd want her to be happy, but she wondered if the whole ruse was the right move on her part. She was smart. She could find a way out of this mess without pretending to be in a relationship with Nathan.

Or maybe she could dodge the gossips altogether and consider selling the inn. She had given that a thought more than a few times since taking over, always feeling stretched beyond her comfort zone in a time when she needed comfort the most. Besides, she could skip town and start over somewhere else where she could fully embrace anonymity again. She stopped herself, realizing she was thinking in circles as she rubbed her forehead.

"Oh no, I've seen that look too many times lately. What's the big deal?" Brooke measured flour before sifting it into her batter.

Erin crossed her arms. Where to start? "I don't know. I guess part of me feels like it's a betrayal to Adam."

"How are you betraying Adam?" Brooke asked. "He's gone."

Erin picked at a cuticle. "I know it's silly, and I feel stupid after hearing that out loud." She was doing it again—overthinking everything.

Brooke paused, making eye contact with Erin. "Unless you're not faking something?"

"No way," Erin blurted.

Brooke studied her under a microscopic glare. Resolved, she shrugged, pouring her batter into a loaf pan. "Okay."

Erin exhaled. "I guess I'll have to put up with being talked about for a few days."

"Don't sound too enthused," Brooke teased. "And hey, you're dodging a bullet with Ted, and at least Nathan is nice to look at."

"That's definitely true."

"Need another courage cookie?" Brooke asked.

Erin shook her head. "In fact, I need to go easy on the sweets." She looked down at her stomach.

"Oh, stop. You're beautiful. Maybe a little crazy but beautiful." Brooke stuck out her tongue, and they both laughed. "Speaking of crazy, don't forget about book club tomorrow night."

Erin *had* almost forgotten. Brooke had convinced her to join a monthly book club with some of the other women in town. She cringed. "I didn't read the book."

"So what? We use the term *book club* very loosely. It's just an excuse to get together to drink wine and gossip." Brooke winked.

Erin chuckled. "I think I can manage that, as long as the gossip doesn't involve me."

"No promises, but we'll try. Now scram, I'm about to add the secret ingredient." She waved Erin away.

"I thought you said we'd never have secrets between us."

"This is different. Besides, don't you have a fake relationship to play up with Mr. Scott? Stop stalling, lady."

Erin laughed, giving her a salute. "Aye, aye!" They said their goodbyes, and Erin walked back to her car, ready to face whatever else fate had in store.

NATHAN WATCHED Erin pull around the back of The Gilded Rose to park. He ignored the nerves firing throughout his body, adrenaline coursing in its wake. Why was he making such a big deal out of this? He'd asked plenty of women out before, and this situation was no different. It was a simple ask. Purely innocent, right?

Even he wasn't buying that his intentions were innocent, considering how hard his heart pounded in his chest.

But it had to be. What other option was there? He was in no position to make any promises beyond the next few days. And while he barely knew Erin, he had an innate feeling he didn't want to string her along like he had with other women before her, intentionally or not. She deserved better than that. He needed to be honest, stressing this was strictly a business proposition. A friend helping a friend. Nothing more.

He needed to make sure *he* remembered that too.

Erin walked toward the front entrance, and Nathan stepped out to greet her. "Just the person I was looking for."

Erin stopped in her tracks as their eyes met. "Is everything okay?"

He'd startled her. Or maybe Nathan wasn't hiding his nerves as well as he thought. He cleared his throat. "Yeah, but I—actually, do you mind sitting with me in the garden?" *Dude, pull yourself together. Simple. Ask.*

Erin hesitated. "Okay." Her skeptical tone did nothing to calm his nerves, only increasing the speed of his jackhammering heart as they walked toward the garden.

He opened the white picket gate for her and followed closely behind. They sat on a bench facing the ocean, the late-day sun casting a warm glow across her perfect skin. The dying light enhanced her sparkling green eyes, and his breath caught in his throat. There was something about her that made him feel at-ease and unhinged at the same time. He'd never felt so conflicted around a woman before. But then again, he'd never met someone after dreaming about them. This was uncharted territory for him in many ways, and he desperately wanted a map.

Normally, he thrived on the unknown, enjoying exploring new places and faces and seeing what may come of it. But this situation left him paralyzed, fearful of doing the wrong thing and hurting her. That was the last thing she deserved after everything she'd been through. She needed someone in her corner, someone to protect her heart from more pain. Was he being selfish in asking this of her?

Her brow wrinkled. "You haven't changed your mind about—"

"No, not at all." He placed a hand on hers as a sign of reassurance. He looked down at their hands as his mind registered how natural it felt to reach for her. The softness of her skin did nothing to help his concentration. He forced himself to continue. "I wanted to ask you something."

"Okay." Her hand twitched under his, and her lips turned up slightly. Her green eyes softened as she looked into his. "Just come out with it. You're making me nervous."

He took a deep breath. *Here goes nothing.* "You know I'm here for TravelCon, right?" She nodded, and he continued. "Well, I'm also being considered for a TV show pilot. I have a meeting with two network executives on Saturday evening, and my new publicist thinks it would help if I brought a date."

"You want me to be your date…to dinner…with TV execs?" She spoke the words slowly, as if they were foreign and she were doing a mental translation to make sense of what he was asking.

"Yeah, if you'd be okay with that." His hand twitched over hers. "Well, actually, my publicist thinks it would be best if I had a girlfriend, but—"

She chuckled. "Well, the whole town already thinks I'm your girlfriend."

"They do?"

Erin nodded. "Our run-in with Ted caused a brushfire with Valerie and the town gossips."

Nathan shifted in his seat. "Huh, who would have thought?"

"You're obviously not from a small town."

"No, definitely not." He chuckled nervously. So, this was what it was like living in a small town. A minor interaction could be taken out of context and blown out of proportion. Although, this time, it wasn't too bad. Wasn't bad at all, actually. When neither of them said anything else, he went out on a limb. "So, is that a yes?"

Erin paused. "I think I can manage that. Your offer to promote the inn still stands, right?"

They were definitely on the same page. Nathan's eyes lit up. "Absolutely. As a matter of fact," he said, pulling his cell phone out of his pocket. "I'll start now."

"Wait." She touched his arm. "Just so we're clear, we're just two professionals helping each other, right?"

"Of course." He swallowed hard. Sparks of electricity coursed through his body from her touch, leaving him feeling less than professional.

Erin removed her hand from his arm, breaking the spell. "Good." She exhaled.

Nathan scanned the courtyard for a good spot for a photo. He felt her eyes on him as he walked the property, lining up the right shot before snapping a picture with his phone to test it out. He took a couple more before calling her over, nodding in approval when he checked his work.

"Here, let's take one together." He leaned in toward her, holding his arm straight in front of them. The sign of the inn was visible in the background behind them, and her proximity was electrifying. *Professional*, he reminded himself.

Although the subtle hint of her coconut shampoo didn't help with that cause.

Nathan wrapped an arm around her before snapping a picture. It felt natural to have her under his arm, and she fit perfectly in the crook of his shoulder. He reluctantly removed his arm before he flipped back to his pictures so they could examine the quick work.

"What do you think?" he asked, flipping through the photos with his thumb, thankful to have something to occupy his hands while he resisted taking her into his arms again. He lingered on the picture of the two of them, which certainly looked more cozy than professional. "Are you okay with this?"

Erin nodded. "They look great."

"I'll go ahead and get these posted. At least that's a start. I'll take some more with my Nikon tomorrow, and I'll highlight the inn on my blog post on Mystic Beach." He furrowed his brow as he typed on his screen, searching for the right words.

"So, how'd you become a travel blogger anyway?"

Nathan looked up from his screen. "I've always loved traveling, and to this day, I have a hard time staying in one place. The fact that I get paid to do it still shocks me." He shrugged. "I fully suspect at some point my luck will run out. Someone younger and hotter will come along and displace me."

"Doubtful," Erin blurted. "I mean, you're talking to television executives. That sounds pretty serious." She pretended to scratch her nose, but Nathan could still see her cheeks turn pink.

He smiled. "Yeah, I guess it is. It's a huge jump for my career if the cards fall right." His eyes lingered on hers for a moment before he turned his attention back to his post.

"Speaking of, as soon as I receive more detail from my publicist about dinner Saturday night, I'll let you know."

"Sounds good. I'll be your Julia Roberts," she said. "Except for the whole hooker part."

"Too bad," he said. Oh God, he'd said that out loud? "Not that—never mind. I'm going to quit while I'm ahead." He felt his ears turn pink. "Here." He motioned for her to look over his shoulder at what he'd put together as a post.

I'm exploring #MysticBeach while in town for #TravelCon and am overwhelmed by the hospitality at The Gilded Rose. Erin, the owner, is a total sweetheart. Your next trip to San Francisco should include this idyllic town and a stay at this beautiful bed and breakfast.

His eyes lingered on the photo he'd taken of the two of them as she read his post. They looked good together. Natural, almost.

She nodded. "That's great. Thank you so much. If your definition of hospitality includes saving the innkeeper from drowning in suds, I'd say that's accurate."

He smiled. "I'm glad I could help. I couldn't tag you. Do you have a profile?"

She grimaced. "I don't do social media." When he blinked at her, she added, "I like to keep my life private."

"You own a business. You should at least have a profile for the inn so people can tag and share pictures of themselves having a great time here, to the envy of their friends and family."

Erin shrugged. "I guess you're right. I just don't want to get all cracked out on my phone, you know? I mean, no offense. It's your livelihood, so it's different." She bit her bottom lip, drawing Nathan's attention to her mouth.

He forced himself to look away from her kissable lips. "None taken." He held up his hands, indicating no harm done. "I need to run an errand, but I can help set you up later if you want. I'll even give you a social media tutorial."

"Receiving a social media tutorial from an expert like you? I'm honored," she joked, placing her hand over her heart for greater effect.

He smiled. "Cool, it's a date—err, I mean, we'll catch up later."

"Sounds good."

"Okay, that's my cue. I've reached my two dumb statements per conversation limit." Did that count as three? He felt like a bumbling idiot as his mind mocked the out-of-character behavior.

Erin laughed. "Enjoy running errands."

"I'll do my best." He smiled, keeping his gaze locked on hers for a beat too long before breaking the spell. He walked toward his car, but not before looking back at her over his shoulder. He'd be lucky to call someone like Erin a girlfriend for real. *It's fake, it's not real.*

But one thing that was real was how off-kilter he felt around this woman in a way he'd never felt before, to the point he was behaving like a teenage boy around the head cheerleader. No woman had ever made him feel more awkward, yet more comfortable to be himself before in his life. He didn't know where it was coming from, but he knew one thing for certain: he wanted to get to know her better.

7

*E*rin tossed and turned, unable to find sleep. She couldn't get Nathan out of her mind, their interactions replaying on an endless loop. The way his face lit up whenever he spoke about his work. How her stomach flip-flopped when they took a picture together and he pulled her close. But the one thing she couldn't shake was the way he'd looked at her, his eyes piercing yet warm, like he could see right through to her very soul. It reminded her of Adam's intense gaze, and she found herself feeling something she hadn't felt in a long time: sexy.

She hadn't been sure if she'd ever feel that way again after Adam died. After all, she felt lucky to have experienced such a great love in her life, as most people searched for a long time for what she and Adam had. And running the inn had proved to be less than glamorous. Most days, she counted herself lucky if she had a chance to put on mascara before noon, usually skipping it altogether. But after spending the day with Nathan, she felt like she still had it. She was beautiful, *au naturel*. And maybe, just maybe, it was possible she'd find love again, which terrified and excited her at the same time. She'd had it in the back of her mind she'd likely move on eventually, but today had caught her off-guard. Nathan was unexpected.

Despite the awakening of her dormant femininity, she couldn't help wondering if it was happening too soon. Was she really ready to take a chance with her heart again? Even if she were ready, there was no way a relationship with someone like Nathan could work. In a few days, he'd be off to a different corner of the world, and she wasn't interested in globetrotting, no matter how smoldering his eyes were or how much he made her skin tingle with desire.

Frustrated, Erin threw back the covers, giving up on sleep. A cup of chamomile tea might help calm her nerves and slow her mind. She placed her feet on the cold floorboards, her toes curling back in protest before she found her slippers to keep them warm. She fumbled with the lamp knob before turning it on, shielding her eyes from the sudden brightness. As her eyes adjusted, she trudged toward her bathrobe hanging on the back of the bathroom door and wrapped it tightly around her body.

As to not disturb her guests, she slowly twisted her doorknob and tip-toed down the stairs toward the kitchen. Before reaching the doorway, she heard shuffling in the kitchen. She stopped dead in her tracks. Her heart raced. Did someone break in? She had, in fact, locked the back door before heading upstairs, right?

Feeling defenseless, she looked around and grabbed the nearest thing she thought might provide some protection: a golf umbrella. Holding it like a baseball bat, she gingerly approached the kitchen, ready to protect her nest as her pulse pounded in her ears. She squinted, bracing herself for the worst before jumping through the doorway, preparing to swing.

"Woah, stop! It's me!" Nathan held his hands and arms over his face in defense.

"Nathan?" She dropped the umbrella to her side. "What are you doing?"

"Couldn't sleep."

She took a deep breath, holding a hand over her chest. "You scared me to death."

He eyed her umbrella. "You're telling me. That thing looks lethal."

She set the umbrella down against a kitchen cabinet. "It's the only thing that was nearby. I thought I'd left the back door unlocked and someone got in."

His arm flinched before he ran his fingers through his hair. "I didn't mean to scare you."

Her pulse slowing back to normal, Erin took a deep breath. "It's okay. I was going to make some tea. Do you want some?"

He nodded. "Sounds good. Have anything to snack on?"

Erin pulled her bathrobe a little tighter. She couldn't help noticing how Nathan's grey-blue eyes sparkled in the dim light of the moon shining through the kitchen window. Instinctively, she turned on a nearby light, causing both of them to squint as they adjusted to the lack of mood lighting.

"Yeah, there's some cookies my friend Brooke made." Erin filled the kettle and turned on the burner, watching the spark ignite the flame as the hum of oscillating fans over the slightly damp floors from the morning's debacle kept them company. She pulled out a plate for the courage cookies before joining Nathan at the kitchen table.

"Why can't you sleep?" he asked.

She shrugged. "Just restless, I guess. You?" She avoided eye contact, afraid he'd be able to tell from one look that he was the reason she felt restless.

"Same." He paused. "I usually have a hard time sleeping before a conference."

"That's understandable. And this is a new environment."

Nathan shook his head. "Thankfully, I don't have a problem sleeping anywhere."

"Oh, right." She laughed nervously. "Part of the job." The kettle whined, and Erin took it off the burner, filling two mugs with hot water. "Chamomile okay?" she asked, and Nathan nodded. She dropped the tea bags in to steep, returning to the table with their respective mugs.

"I looked earlier, and my post about the inn is getting a lot of activity," he said.

"I hope something comes from it." She drizzled honey into her mug and stirred the hot water. She couldn't bear it if this place failed. She felt like she'd be letting her family and the town down to some degree. But with mounting debt and slow bookings, it felt like failure was inevitable. If she were going to stay afloat, something had to change, fast, or she'd have no choice but to consider selling. She really didn't want to throw in the white towel of defeat.

"What's wrong?"

"Nothing," she replied too quickly, resting her spoon on the lip of the cookie plate.

He eyed her suspiciously. "Your poker face is terrible."

Erin always considered her poker face masterful. Someone had to really know her to see through her facade. Perhaps it wasn't as good as she once believed. Either that, or Nathan was acutely aware of her minor tells.

She sighed. "Bookings have been a little light lately, that's all. I'm sure things will pick up." They had to.

He nodded before taking a bite of cookie, his expression turning toward total bliss as it crumbled over his tongue. "This is amazing. It tastes like a warm, cozy blanket on a cold day." His brow furrowed. "How is that possible?"

"My best friend made them, and even I don't know how she does it. She always kicks me out of the kitchen before adding her secret ingredient."

He examined the cookie. "Remarkable." He took another bite, relishing the taste. "They taste like...home."

She shrugged. "Funny, they taste like home to you but courage to me." She watched as he averted his gaze, a micro-expression of pain flashing across his face before he hid behind his mug. Guilt rushed over her for making him feel uncomfortable. "Did I say something wrong?"

He shook his head and took another bite, avoiding any explanation. She examined him, realizing he'd behaved similarly earlier when she'd brought up his parents. Vacillating between curiosity and not wanting to pry, she decided to go for it. She broke off a piece of cookie to give her the extra boost she'd need to ask what was really on her mind. "You know, you never answered my question earlier."

"Which one?"

"About your parents." She paused. "What happened to them?"

Nathan shifted in his chair. "It's a long story."

"I've got time. I only have to be up in about five hours to make breakfast." She smiled, pretending to examine her invisible watch. She could practically hear her mother nagging in her ear about manners and being nosey, which gave her pause. "You don't have to tell me if you don't want to."

Nathan looked into her eyes, the intensity of his gaze palpable. "It's really not that big of a deal." He broke their connection, looking down at his mug as he drummed his fingers against it. Erin waited silently, giving him the space he needed to say whatever he wanted. He sighed. "My mother left when I was a boy because I had—I was really ill, and I guess she couldn't handle it. My dad and I moved in with Frances after that, and he got really depressed. He turned to the booze for comfort and ended up killing himself in the process. It's just been me and Frances ever since."

Erin's heart sank. "Wow, I'm so sorry."

He shrugged. "It's alright."

But it wasn't. She could see the pain in his eyes as he talked about his mother walking out on him and even more disdain for his father, who turned to alcohol for comfort despite his feigning nonchalance. Erin could only imagine how it must have felt being abandoned by the two people who should be trusted the most in a child's life. She instinctively placed a hand on his forearm, waiting for Nathan to meet her gaze. "You know none of that was your fault, right?" His muscles twitched under her hand, drawing her attention to the warmth of his skin.

"Yeah, I know." He broke their connection, taking a sip of his tea and averting his gaze. They sat in silence, the ghosts of his past haunting the room. She couldn't help feeling like he was saying that because it was expected. A knee-jerk, socially acceptable, canned response.

He straightened in his chair. "I just thought of something."

"What?" Erin broke off another piece of cookie. It wasn't lost on her that he'd changed the subject, shutting the door on his past. But she wasn't about to pry further, feeling like she'd already slightly overstepped.

"Have you thought about partnering with some of the local businesses? That might help drive some traffic and increase bookings. Maybe you could offer a combined package of some sort."

"That's a great idea," she mumbled. Why hadn't she thought of that herself? She cut her mind off from chastising herself.

"We're close enough to Sonoma and Napa, right? Are there any other wineries nearby?"

She gave it some thought. "There's Cheshire Moon Winery a few miles down the PCH."

"Great." He added a little more honey to his tea. "Are you busy tomorrow?"

She ran down a mental checklist in her head. "Just the usual. Why?"

He smiled. "We should go check it out. I've got a cocktail reception for TravelCon in the evening, but otherwise, I'm free."

Before Erin could protest, a simple, "Okay," popped out of her mouth. She attempted to cover her surprise by bringing her mug to her lips, taking a long sip of tea.

"Okay, it's a date." He smiled before yawning. "And on that note, I think I need to try to get some more shut eye."

Erin nodded in agreement. "I should probably try to sleep too." She reached for their dishes to put them in the sink.

"Here, let me," he said, their hands grazing as they both reached for his mug. His warm touch electrified her skin, and she raised her eyes to meet his intense gaze. If she didn't know better, she'd think his blue gray eyes appeared stormy. Hungry with need. She licked her lips, and he swallowed hard. She felt magnetically drawn to him, unable to move her hand as she relished his touch. He leaned in slightly, and her heart jumped into her throat. Her eyes slowly closed, anticipating what his next move would be. Was she ready for this? She'd be lying if she said she wasn't a little curious about how it would feel to kiss him.

He cleared his throat, and her eyes popped back open. He stepped back, relinquishing the mug and the spell he'd cast on her. "Goodnight, Erin," he murmured before ascending toward his room.

"'Night." Slightly dazed, Erin took the mugs toward the sink, hand washing them before putting them on a rack to dry. Was her mind playing tricks on her, or was he about to kiss her? She'd had just enough courage coursing through her veins that she would have let him. It was shocking to her to feel the pulses of desire for someone she'd just met, but what surprised her more was the sinking feeling of disappointment when he pulled away.

She shook her head and turned off the light in the kitchen before heading toward her room. Those cookies sure worked in mysterious ways.

HE'D ALMOST KISSED HER.

Nathan sat in the garden overlooking the bay, yawning after a restless night. Erin was wrapping up a couple of things before they headed out toward Cheshire Moon Winery, and he'd decided to get some air before they spent the rest of the day together. So far, no amount of sunshine or picturesque views of the bay were helping to quell his desire. He'd tossed and turned all night, unable to get Erin out of his mind. Her warm eyes, her soft skin, and the way she'd bitten her bottom lip kept dancing through his head. His instincts had kicked in, making it nearly impossible to leave the kitchen last night before they took hold completely. And now he was going to spend the entire day with her and attempt to keep his hands to himself.

He was definitely in trouble.

Last night in the kitchen, something magical transpired between them. He felt an odd connection to this woman, finding it incomprehensible that they'd just met. Something about her made it easy to open up about his past and share parts of himself he'd never wanted to talk about before. He hated feeling vulnerable and tried his best to avoid being placed in situations where he wasn't in control. But something about Erin made him feel safe, accepted somehow, and it didn't hurt that she was gorgeous.

However, he couldn't lose sight of what brought him to Mystic Beach to begin with. He had a job to do, a TV contract to earn, and then he'd be on his way to some far-off part of the globe. Alone. He needed to keep his eye on the prize, and not the one currently puttering in the kitchen.

The French door opened, causing him to turn around.

"Okay, I'm ready," Erin said, running fingers through her long blonde hair.

Nathan's breath caught in his throat. Her eyes sparkled in the midday sun, and her complexion was slightly flushed after quickly wrapping up her last-minute chores. She wore a pair of jeans that hugged her figure in all the right places and had paired them with a white boatneck top that revealed her delicate collarbone. His mouth went dry as he thought about trailing kisses along her neck. He swallowed hard, forcing himself to focus.

"Great, my car is just over there." He motioned with the phone in his hands. "I'll drive if you'll be my navigator?"

"Sounds like a plan."

As they walked toward his car, he let her go ahead of him, guiding her with a gently placed hand on the small of her back. As his skin burned with desire from touching her, he quickly removed his hand and adjusted his sunglasses. *Stay focused*. He opened the car door for her, watching her climb in before walking around to the driver's seat. As she plugged the address for the winery into GPS and he forced himself to take shallow breaths, her jasmine and amber perfume intoxicated him. He welcomed the distraction of the straight-laced voice from the GPS as it spouted directions.

"Good day so far?" Nathan asked as an ice breaker.

"Yeah, nothing too exciting, which is always a good thing in this business," Erin said. "Everyone thinks owning a bed and breakfast is so glamorous until you have to plunge weird objects from your toilet."

"Sounds like you're speaking from personal experience."

"You have no idea."

Nathan chuckled. "Well, for what it's worth, you seem to be very good at what you do. I can see why your aunt trusted you with it." He turned toward the Pacific Coast Highway and merged with traffic.

"Thank you. Sometimes, I feel like I'm faking it, but every day seems easier than the last. That's progress, right?" She smiled.

He nodded. "One day at a time." He knew this mantra too well, having lived one day at a time for so long, waiting to see if that day would be the one he'd receive a heart. He'd worried that his heart would give out before he got the call, but fortunately, it all worked out in the end. He'd vowed to never take another day for granted again, knowing exactly how fragile life was.

"Your conference kicks off tonight, right?" Erin asked, bringing him back to the present.

He nodded. "There's a cocktail reception tonight and a full day of sessions tomorrow, which gives me a little more time to prepare for my panel discussion on Saturday." It would be the first panel discussion since he received his heart, and Nathan was thankful for the confidence of knowing his new ticker would be able to keep up with him.

"That's exciting," she said. "What's the topic?"

"Affiliate marketing." He cleared his throat. "I'm a little nervous, to be honest." He flashed her a thin smile.

"I'm sure you have no need to be," she said, placing a reassuring hand on his forearm. The jolt he felt from her warm touch radiated to his shoulder, causing him to jerk the wheel toward the edge of the road. The two of them experienced slight turbulence from rolling over rumble strips before he corrected into the right lane.

"Sorry 'bout that," he said, heat rising to his cheeks. They sat in silence for a few beats before Nathan turned on the radio while he focused on getting them there in one piece.

Fortunately, the drive wasn't too long, and after a few turns down a handful of one-lane roads, the sign for Cheshire Moon greeted them. Nathan drove slowly as they wound their way around the vineyard nestled between sweeping ocean views and the Santa Cruz mountains. The sun highlighted the ripening fruit on Chardonnay and Pinot Noir vines, which would be ready for harvest in about a month based on what he could see. They parked near the main tasting room and restaurant, which featured a sweeping deck overlooking the vines and the ocean.

Despite the natural beauty around them, Nathan couldn't take his eyes off Erin as she closed her eyes and tilted her head toward the sky, relishing the warmth of the sun. She smiled as she moaned, thoroughly enjoying the fresh air and coastal breeze as the stress from the inn melted away. "Good idea," she said, casting an appreciative glance at Nathan.

He found himself feeling jealous of the sun, which so easily touched and warmed her skin. The sound of her appreciative moan from taking in their surroundings stirred desire within him. His mouth went dry and he swallowed hard, reminding himself they were there to forge a partnership with the winery, not each other.

"Ready to taste some wine?" he asked. When she nodded, he held out his elbow for her to grab, and she placed a delicate hand on his arm. Clearly, he'd become a glutton for punishment, feeling tortured every time she touched him but unable to stop. Besides, he didn't need to act on every impulse. He could practice restraint. And while his imagination ran wild thinking about Erin moaning from more than just the sun tickling her skin, he vowed to continue being a gentleman.

They ascended a handful of steps toward the main tasting room, and Nathan, true to his gentlemanly commitment, held the door open for Erin and kept his hands to himself as he followed behind her.

The tasting room had wood-paneled vaulted ceilings that added warmth and depth to the space. One wall was lined with a long granite-covered bar holding wine glasses ready to be filled with vintages old and new. A few casks lined another wall, which Nathan suspected was more for ambiance than practicality, and a picture window overlooked the vineyard, allowing ample natural light to shine through.

An older woman wearing a light pink sweater set with her hair pulled back in a twist greeted them from behind the bar and asked if they would like to try some wine. They nodded, and she pulled out a menu for them to browse.

Nathan watched Erin pull her hair to one side as she glanced over the tasting menu, revealing her delicate neck. He inched closer, trying his best to resist tasting what he was really craving by putting his attention on the menu.

"When should I ask about partnering?" Erin mumbled through the side of her mouth.

"Easy, tiger. It'll happen naturally," he said, placing an assuring hand on her back. As his mind registered the warmth of her body under his fingertips, he immediately removed the hand and ran it through his hair. He noticed their companion was wearing a name tag. "Which one is your favorite, Cassandra?"

She smiled. "They're all good, but I might be a little biased." She leaned in conspiratorially. "My grandson is the winemaker."

Nathan grinned. "Lovely. So, Cheshire Moon is family-owned and operated?"

"Oh, yes," Cassandra said. "Dating back to my late husband, Sal. God rest his soul." Cassandra made a cross over her chest. "We're fortunate to have had children who wanted to take part in the family business and provide fresh ideas to help us continue to grow. Pun intended." She chuckled at her own joke. "My daughter-in-law has a background in marketing, and she's recently expanded our operation to include weddings and special events."

"That's fantastic," Nathan said. "Erin here owns a bed and breakfast in Mystic Beach."

"How nice," Cassandra said. "Which one, dear?"

"The Gilded Rose," Erin said.

Confusion spread across Cassandra's face. "I don't think I've heard of that one before."

"The Gilded Rose has been family-owned and operated for years, just like your business," Nathan said. "In fact, Erin recently took over for her late aunt."

"I'm so sorry for your loss, dear," Cassandra said, placing a comforting hand on Erin's arm.

"It's okay." Erin shifted her stance. "Actually, I'm interested in hearing more about your weddings and special events. Do you have a—"

"Oh, of course," Cassandra said, the proverbial light bulb flashing. "How long have you two been engaged?"

"That's not—" Erin started.

"We're not—" Nathan added, and he and Erin looked at each other and smiled.

"No?" Cassandra asked, to which both Erin and Nathan shook their heads. "I could have sworn you two were."

"What makes you say that?" Erin asked.

Cassandra shrugged. "You look like you belong together. There's something there." She pointed her finger back and forth between Nathan and Erin. "Something that reminds me of Sal and me when we were younger. Gosh, we couldn't keep our hands off each other." She looked off into the distance.

Nathan watched Erin through the corner of his eye as she blushed, pushing a loose strand of hair behind her ear. Was Cassandra right? He certainly felt a pull, an unexplainable tug, whenever he was around Erin. He'd never been one to believe in fate or having a soulmate whom he was destined to be with. But the connection he felt building certainly felt unlike anything he'd ever experienced.

Cassandra blushed, coming out of her reverie. "Oh, I'm so sorry. You two wanted to try some wine."

Erin nodded. "We do, and I'm also wondering if you have any hotels or bed and breakfasts you partner with for your special events and weddings?" She said the words quickly, as if she were afraid of not getting them all out.

"Yes, we have a preferred vendor list we've started building," Cassandra said.

"That's great. How can I get on it?" Erin asked.

Nathan watched Erin fidget and take a deep breath. She was so clearly out of her comfort zone, and he admired her courage.

"Do you have a card handy? If so, I can take it to my daughter-in-law and get you on the list."

Erin nodded, pulling a card from her purse and handing it to Cassandra, who looked at it fondly. "I love the idea of families helping families." She beamed.

Erin exhaled, her shoulders visibly relaxing. Nathan took the liberty of ordering both pinot noir and chardonnay tastings, and Cassandra poured generously, suggesting they take their glasses onto the back deck with a wink.

"You did great," Nathan assured Erin as soon as they were out of earshot. They settled at a high-top table overlooking the thriving grape vines as the sun gently warmed their skin, a perfect balance to the cool breeze from the bay in the distance.

"What a rush." She smiled. "You were great too, by the way. I had no idea it would be that easy."

"Our minds often make mountains out of molehills. At least, that's what Frances always told me growing up."

Erin paused. "Funny, my dad used to say the exact same thing."

"Smart man." Nathan watched as Erin turned her attention toward the vineyard, her hair blowing gently in the breeze. When she flashed him a warm smile, he questioned if sticking to his morals and not making a move made him a smart man too. He was the kind of guy who lived in the moment and normally wouldn't hesitate to go after what he wanted. But Erin was different. Knowing she'd overcome heartbreak after an incomprehensible loss made him want to handle her with care. However, with every warm smile and fleeting touch, he was finding it damn near impossible to continue doing the right thing.

Nathan raised a glass. "Cheers to your new partnership." They clinked, neither one looking away as they took a sip. Heat from her gaze penetrated his resolve, and he set down his glass. He was ready to throw caution to the wind and be stupid. Besides, after everything she'd been through, Erin probably wasn't looking for anything serious either.

Only one way to find out.

"I hope something comes from it." She wrapped two fingers around the stem of her wine glass as she looked down at the table.

He reached over and gently raised her chin until their eyes met. "For what it's worth, I can see why your aunt trusted you with the inn. I think you're a natural."

"Really?"

He nodded, cradling her face in his hand. He leaned in

slightly, testing the waters to see if she'd flinch backward, but she didn't move. Taking that as a green light, he inched closer to her, his heart banging rapidly in his chest as he prepared to—

Her phone rang.

At first, neither of them looked away. But curiosity got the best of Erin, and she said it could be something important at the inn.

Nathan reluctantly dropped his hand from her face and took a big sip from his glass as she answered the phone. He silently cursed whoever was on the opposite end of the phone. Their timing flat out sucked. His pulse steadied as the moment completely passed, the energy shifting away from lust.

"Sorry, I'll be there in twenty." She hung up, her eyes wide with panic. "I completely forgot about Ted coming to assess the damage this afternoon. I need to get back."

"He's waiting there now?" he asked, and she nodded. "Okay, we better move." He pushed back his chair and she did the same, and they walked through the tasting room. Erin paused, buying two bottles of wine, explaining that she'd promised to bring some for her book club meeting that evening. Nathan insisted on carrying the bottles to the car.

"Do you mind hanging around while he's there?" Erin asked.

"Not at all."

"It won't interfere with your cocktail reception, will it?"

He shook his head, opening her car door. "It doesn't start until six, but even so, this is more important."

Erin looked at him before getting in the car. "Thanks. You're a really good…friend."

There it was. The kiss of death. His insides twisted at the word. Was his mind playing tricks on him, or did her inflection turn up slightly at the word, insinuating a quasi-question? No. Clearly, she was telling him that's where they stood, and he needed to take it at face value. Besides, who was he kidding thinking something could actually happen between them? He'd be gone in a few days, and the last thing he needed to do was make a mess before he left. She deserved more than that. More than him.

That call came at the right time after all.

He nodded in response to her words and mumbled, "No problem," before closing her car door and getting into the driver's seat. Once they were both strapped in, he sped back toward the inn, both of them silent for most of the drive.

8

---

*N*athan approached the check-in table to obtain his schedule for the next three days. It had been a while since he'd made it to an industry conference, and the buzz of excitement in the air was contagious. He felt his spirits lifting, and he looked forward to immersion in industry trends for the weekend. His nerves fired to life, which had nothing to do with a certain blonde he couldn't get out of his mind.

Keeping up the ruse of being Erin's boyfriend in front of Ted was more difficult after their afternoon at the winery. He hoped he was still a convincing actor despite trying his best to maintain a distance between him and Erin. And Ted wasn't the only one who booked it out of there quickly. He needed to put some distance between him and Erin too, especially after she took his hand between both of hers and thanked him profusely for protecting her from creepy Ted. His skin ached from her touch, causing desire to threaten to boil over. He hoped he hadn't left too abruptly.

Erin was absolutely infectious. He couldn't explain it, but every time he was around her, he felt a homecoming, a magnetism drawing him toward his complementary polarity. He'd always repelled women when things got to a certain point. He'd been afraid of getting too close. And despite the attraction he felt for Erin, he couldn't let it go past the thin veil of professionalism, or *friendship*, still hanging over both of them.

No matter how much she haunted his dreams.

Nathan exchanged pleasantries with an older woman who handed him his badge and schedule as she checked him in. She nodded approvingly at the panelist ribbon attached to the bottom of his badge and wished him luck. He needed it for more than just his talk on Saturday. He hoped that luck would carry over for his dinner meeting with television executives too. All he could do was be himself and demonstrate how he was a sure thing. He felt more confident knowing he'd have Erin there acting as his good luck charm. Or secret weapon. If keeping his hands to himself didn't kill him first.

He needed a drink.

Nathan entered the expo hall and found the nearest open bar. He stood in line waiting for a drink, overhearing the buzz of networking and schmoozing around him.

"Panelist, huh?"

"Yeah, I'm on the panel for Affiliate Marketing in our industry, for better or worse." Nathan shrugged.

"I'm Paul Fitzgerald." The man held out his hand for Nathan to shake. "You're the Wander-Lust guy, right?"

"Yeah, that's me." Nathan blushed. It wasn't too often he heard his social media identity out loud, and somehow, it sounded a little ridiculous to him now. "Although it seems like a lot of people these days are using that schtick."

Paul looked sheepish. "Myself included. But you set the bar, man. It's all your fault."

Nathan chuckled. "It's always my fault." He knew Paul

was right. Part of what made Nathan famous in the travel blogging community was he was the first guy to play up his sex appeal in his posts. Most of his pictures were shirtless, and his female followers often posted derogatory comments asking for more skin whenever he did post something with clothes on. There were many guys who'd followed his lead since, but he was the first. A true pioneer. Accept no imitations.

Some days, he felt like a traveling social media gigolo since he made more money with his clothes off than on. But ever since his surgery, he'd been reluctant to post any more shirtless photos. He didn't want the world to see the scar on his chest, knowing it wouldn't be hard to piece together what happened. He hoped through earning the TV contract, he could reinvent himself and segue into a new phase of his career, ideally with all his clothes on. Besides, there were plenty of guys like Paul who would gladly take the baton when he handed it over.

Paul scanned their surroundings. "Seen any hotties yet?" Before Nathan could answer, he continued, "I love these conferences. Free booze and plenty of hot women who are from out of town and ready to make bad choices."

Nathan shook his head. "Can't say I've paid much attention."

"Yeah, but you just got here, right?" Paul looked around as they inched closer to the bar, his neck craning to spot any unsuspecting prey. "Check out that redhead at three o'clock."

Nathan looked discreetly at a statuesque redhead wearing a V-neck red dress that hugged her curves, leaving very little left to imagination. Her full lips were coated in red lipstick to match her dress, and she tossed her hair over a shoulder, smiling in their direction. He had to admit she looked good, but it also appeared like she knew it.

"Now there's a woman ready to make bad decisions." Paul

looked at the woman like a gazelle he was ready to pounce on and devour. She held his gaze and smiled, looking away and back again, her eyes then lingering on Nathan. "I love those redheads." Paul licked his lips.

"Trouble," Nathan said. "Trust me. They're all nuts." He'd had one too many experiences with gorgeous redheads like the woman at three o'clock to know better than to play with that kind of fire again. Besides, she couldn't hold a candle to Erin.

"I like a little crazy, though," Paul said. "Keeps it interesting."

"Yeah, until they set your clothes on fire and throw them out a window."

"That happened to you?" Paul asked.

Nathan nodded. "Once. In Phuket of all places."

Paul's face lit up. "Dude, you're a legend. Let me buy you a drink."

Nathan laughed. "They're free."

Paul smiled. "Precisely." They reached the bartender and ordered a light beer and whiskey and soda. "Cheers, mate," Paul said, clinking his longneck against Nathan's cup before taking a long pull.

Nathan watched Paul make eyes at the redhead, or was his attention now on the brunette next to her? He couldn't keep up. Nor did he want to.

"Hey, be my wingman?" Paul elbowed him. "Let's go talk to those beauties."

Before Nathan could respond, Paul walked toward the two women. Nathan rolled his eyes and followed behind. If anything, he didn't want to miss the train as it derailed and crashed.

"Good evening, ladies." Paul's tone was smooth. "I'm Paul, and I think you need to know me."

"Oh, really? What gives you that impression?" The redhead placed a hand on her hip.

"The way you were looking at me from across the room. I know, my magnetism is palpable and undeniable. What's your name, sheila?"

Is this guy for real?

"Heather."

"Melissa," the brunette said simultaneously.

"Perfect." Paul grinned widely as he bared his teeth as though ready to sink them into his prey.

Nathan hid a smile behind his drink, taking a sip while scanning the room. Clearly, Paul didn't need him, and frankly, he wasn't interested in a random hook-up. Normally, he would find someone like Paul at a conference and they would team up and find women to keep them company for the weekend. But participating in it now felt a little too sleazy for comfort.

"Mate?" Paul asked.

"Sorry. Hi, I'm Nathan." He smiled and nodded a hello at Heather and Melissa.

"You bored?" Heather asked.

"No, how could I be with you two around?" Nathan said robotically as he scanned the room. The words tasted funny rolling off his tongue. His heart definitely wasn't in it.

Melissa rolled her eyes.

"Sorry, ladies. My friend is acting a little strange." Paul wrapped an arm around each of them. "Here, let me buy you a drink."

Heather laughed. "They're free."

"Whatever." Paul led them toward the open bar.

"I'll catch up with you later," Nathan said, and Paul winked at him over Melissa's shoulder. Nathan exhaled a sigh of relief being away from them and couldn't help feeling like he'd dodged a bullet. But it wasn't lost on him how out of character his reaction was. He'd definitely changed after going under the knife, having lived on the brink of death for so long. Perhaps his heart had changed during the transplant, bringing what was truly important into sharper focus. Or perhaps the whiskey was a little stronger than he thought and he'd better switch to water.

Sucking on an ice cube, he perused the rows of tables with exhibitors showcasing the latest gadgets for travel. The highlights included a suitcase that rolled on its own and was controlled by a smartphone app, a new digital camera with more compact, higher definition lenses, and clip-on camera lenses and tripods for smartphones. While the latest technology impressed him, he didn't see anything he couldn't live without, and before long, he found it hard to breathe. The desperation in the room was suffocating, emanating from exhibitors and attendees looking to sell themselves in various capacities. He had to get out of there.

He downed the remainder of his drink, crunching another piece of ice as he threw the cup away and headed back toward the inn.

It was bound to be a long weekend.

SHE'D CALLED HIM A *FRIEND*.

Erin pretended to listen to Brooke as they drove together. Brooke had volunteered to pick her up for the evening's festivities, insisting Erin cut loose and drink at least two glasses of wine with the girls. After today, she likely wouldn't argue; she needed to numb her mind from replaying how Nathan tenderly touched her face when they were at the winery. How he looked at her with burning desire. How he'd almost kissed her.

How she almost let him.

Her mind had a hard time keeping up with the barrage. On one hand, she surprised herself by feeling sparks of desire for a man who wasn't Adam. She'd feared those parts of her had withered from neglect, blown out to sea by the diablo winds. But those winds had diabolical plans of their own, blowing Nathan into town. He'd sparked and fueled flames of desire, and they threatened to spread wildfires through every fiber of her being. Those womanly parts of her were very much alive, and Nathan was their defibrillator.

On the other hand, he'd be gone in a few days, and she'd just pieced her heart back together. She was too fragile to consider succumbing to lust with him without monumental consequences. The best thing she could do was force distance between them, and she must have known on a subconscious level the word friend would be like a cold bucket of ice water for both of them. He'd kept a respectable distance the rest of the afternoon, which was for the best, despite her insides threatening to reach out and ask him to pick up where they left off before Ted called.

Yes, *at least* two glasses of wine were warranted.

"And then the purple elephant told the green tiger to pull his trunk."

"What?" Erin asked.

"Oh, so *you are* listening to me." Brooke pulled into a parking spot. "Just double checking."

"Sorry," Erin mumbled. "It's been a long day."

"Wouldn't have anything to do with a certain sexy blogger, would it?"

Erin blushed. "Nope."

Brooke rolled her eyes. "Whatever you say." They both got out of her car.

"What do you call this again?" Erin asked as she and Brooke walked toward the front door of Celestial Books and Brew.

"It's the Friday Eve Book Club," Brooke said proudly. "Heavy on the Friday Eve festivities, light on the books." She winked.

"Think this is okay?" Erin asked, holding out the bottles of red and white she'd picked up at the winery that afternoon.

Brooke nodded. "That one is Denise's favorite." She pointed to the red. "Smooth move, already earning brownie points." Brooke pushed open the front door to the shop, revealing a mix of new age books, crystals, and various accoutrement to the right, and nag champa incense wafted in their faces. A few tables and chairs lined the left side of the room, including one set up for fortune telling with a royal purple velvet tablecloth. Straight back is where they found Denise, who looked up from behind the dessert case next to the industrial-sized coffee machine and smiled.

"Finally," Denise said. She greeted them warmly with hugs and a single kiss on the cheek. "Lovely seeing you both." Denise had crystal blue eyes and straight ebony hair. Her bright red lips were like tiny flames against her porcelain skin. She reminded Erin of a Hollywood star.

"I brought wine," Erin offered, holding up the bottles.

Denise studied them. "Did you put her up to this?" she asked Brooke, who shook her head. "You sure know how to make friends quickly." Denise looped an arm around Erin's elbow. "Come, let me introduce you to everyone."

Denise led them toward the back deck where three other women sat in Adirondack chairs around a fire pit. They introduced themselves as Margot, Laurie, and Kendall. String lights added ambience to the space, framing the area above the smoldering fire. Everyone seemed really nice, which made Erin relax. She always felt awkward around new people and absolutely loathed small talk. She'd rather stick a fork in her eye than talk about the weather. Despite no one really caring about the weather, it always made its way into polite conversation.

"How about that warm breeze today?" Laurie's blue-green eyes sparkled in the firelight.

"Laurie, no one cares about the weather. Have a drink," Denise said. Erin smiled, feeling as if Denise had read her mind.

"Well, I for one enjoyed it," Kendall said to Laurie. "It made for a great day of surfing."

"Good waves today?" Margot asked and Kendall nodded as she pulled her long blonde waves into a messy bun.

"Sometime, you need to teach me," Brooke said. "I'd love to get out on the surf."

"Yeah, if you can take a break from conjuring magic in your kitchen long enough to enjoy some sunshine," Denise teased.

"You *are* looking a little pale," Kendall said to Brooke, cringing a bit.

"If you two would bake on your own, maybe I would be able to work on my tan instead." Brooke motioned to Erin and Denise. She supplied baked goods for both of their businesses. Happily, of course, but apparently to the detriment of her tan.

Denise shrugged. "But you're so good at it. Why reinvent the wheel?"

"Yeah, we wouldn't want to steal your thunder," Erin teased.

"I like her." Denise pointed her thumb at Erin. "You'll fit in just fine with this motley crew."

Margot poured glasses of wine for everyone, and Laurie took the plastic wrap off the cheese platter on a nearby table. Kendall passed glasses around until everyone had what they wanted.

"Cheers," Kendall said.

"Happy Friday Eve," Margot said, the fire reflecting in her horn-rimmed glasses. Everyone clinked their glasses and sipped.

"What's up with the lack of testosterone in this town?" Kendall asked.

"We're in the middle of a man drought. Have been for years," Denise said.

"I am *so* ready for it to rain good men," Margot mused. They all laughed.

"Yeah, the mayor is on some campaign to increase tourism and asked that hot blogger to do a feature." Laurie snapped her fingers as if it would help her think more clearly. "What's his name?"

"Nathan?" Erin asked.

"Yes, that's it—Nathan." Laurie pointed at Erin. "Do you know him?"

"He's staying at her inn," Brooke volunteered.

"Okay, please tell me. Does he look as hot in person as he does online?" Laurie asked.

"Have you seen him shirtless yet?" Denise asked.

"Oh, you mean Nathan Scott?" Kendall asked. "I follow him on social media."

"Keep up, Kendall." Denise snapped her fingers at her. "Shake the seaweed out of your beautiful head."

Kendall stuck out her tongue at Denise. "I thought you looked familiar," Kendall said to Erin. "I saw you on his feed today." She pulled her phone out of a brown canvas satchel.

"Let me see." Laurie peered over Kendall's shoulder as she scrolled to find the picture.

"Here." Kendall held up her phone for everyone to see.

"I can't see that well. Hang on, let me clean my glasses." Margot used her shirt to wipe fingerprints off her lenses.

"Pass it around," Denise said.

"Me first." Laurie grabbed the phone. She examined the photo. "Wow, you two look cozy." She grinned at Erin.

Erin shrugged, heat flushing her cheeks. "Thanks?"

"Girl, why are you here instead of staring at that fine specimen?" Denise asked.

"He's in town for a conference," Brooke said.

Erin gave Brooke a look of appreciation, knowing she was probably trying to keep her from feeling put on the spot. "Yeah, he hasn't been around much."

"But she *is* going to dinner with him Saturday night," Brooke said.

"What? How'd you get so lucky?" Kendall playfully pushed Erin's arm.

"Laurie, stop hogging that phone and pass it here," Denise demanded.

Erin turned a darker shade of crimson as she looked at Brooke. "Thanks a lot." Brooke shrugged. "I think you need to be cut off," Erin teased, reaching for her friend's glass. So much for not putting her on the spot.

"I'm waiting," Kendall said.

Erin realized her new crew would not take silence for an answer. "He has an important dinner meeting Saturday evening, so he agreed to promote my inn in exchange for me accompanying him to it." She took a big sip from her glass, hoping that would be the end of it. But they hung on her every word, waiting for more detail. "What?"

"That's it?" Denise said. "And we were just starting to become good friends."

Erin laughed nervously. "Yeah, that's it, I promise. Why, is there something I should know?"

"Let me top off your glass," Laurie offered. Erin held it out for her to pour more wine. "You know he has a bit of a…reputation."

"What do you mean?" Erin asked.

"What she means to say is, you know he's a player, right?" Kendall said.

Erin's heart sank at Kendall's words. How could that possibly be true? He'd been nothing but a gentleman to her so far, and she certainly didn't get the impression it was a ruse to seduce her. But how well did she know him anyway? They'd only spent, what, a couple of days together? It takes a lot longer than that to get to know someone. And Kendall clearly followed him closely on social media. Erin couldn't help wondering how many women Kendall had seen Nathan with around the globe. She felt her insides twist into knots.

"Just be careful," Margot said.

"It's just dinner." Erin shrugged. "What's the harm in that?" She knew even as she said the words that she was trying to convince herself more than anyone else. That certainly proved she wasn't ready to feel so vulnerable yet, and she needed to keep her distance for sheer self-preservation.

Denise studied her. "You two have a connection. I can see it in your eyes."

Erin wasn't sure what to say.

"You have more to gain than you think. Just be careful," Denise warned.

"Okay." Were all the women in this town gifted with second sight, or did she suddenly become transparent? She felt relieved when Laurie told a story about her latest real estate client from hell, taking Erin out of the hot seat.

Over a handful of bottles of wine, they spent the rest of the evening musing about local gossip and coming up with possible solutions to the man drought, with no mention of fine literature at all.

9

Nathan dreamed about her again. They were walking along the same cliffside at sunset, her hand in his as he followed her to their lookout point. She turned to him, pressing her body against his, and opened her mouth to speak. Instead of a beautiful timber emitting from her lips, her mouth rang like a telephone.

Startled, Nathan realized his phone was ringing. It was Coco.

"Darling, did I wake you?"

"It's fine." He rubbed his eyes and cleared his throat. "What's up?"

"I just got an email from Jeff's assistant, and there was a scheduling conflict. He wants to move dinner to tonight. Simon's assistant is also on the thread and said the change works with his schedule. I'm calling to make sure it's okay with you."

"Tonight?"

"Yes, keep up darling." Nathan heard her snap her fingers.

He groaned. "Okay." He put her on speaker phone and sat up, drinking a glass of water from his bedside.

"Will you be able to make that work or not?"

He gulped. "I don't have a choice, do I?"

"You're cranky in the morning."

Well, you woke me up before I could kiss my dream girl. What did you expect? "Sorry. Yes, I will make that work. Are the rest of the details the same?"

He heard her typing in the background. "I'll confirm it and let you know."

"Sounds good." He could smell the faint scent of coffee and bacon, and his stomach growled to life.

"I saw your social media post from Wednesday," Coco said. "Is that who you're bringing to dinner?"

Nathan immediately transported back to that photographic moment in his mind's eye. The electricity between them, the magnetism of her smile, and the faint smell of her coconut shampoo. It took everything in him not to wrap his arms around her and kiss her in that moment and every moment since.

"Hello?"

"That's Erin. She's the innkeeper where I'm staying."

"She's perfect. Very girl-next-door. The executives will eat her up."

"They better not," he blurted.

"Ooh, possessive, are we?"

Nathan shook his head. What had gotten into him? "What I meant to say was—"

She cut him off. "No, I think I got it. I like the sound of this."

"I didn't say anything."

"You didn't have to. Anyway, I'll let you know once everything is confirmed. Bye-bye!" She hung up.

Nathan looked at the black screen and chuckled. Coco reminded him so much of his aunt Frances. No wonder they were friends.

He stretched before walking toward the bathroom to shave and get ready for the day. He did a mental rundown of his talking points for the panel discussion taking place that afternoon as he brushed his teeth. While shaving, his thoughts wandered to dinner. He'd learned a long time ago that flexibility was key in his industry. Flights were delayed and sometimes canceled. Occasionally, he'd lose his reservation at a hotel due to glitches in computer systems. Weather often threw a wrench in the best laid out plans. Needless to say, he'd become very fluid over the years, out of necessity and survival. Not everyone shared the same fluidity though, and he hoped Erin would be able to adapt to this change.

Nathan realized he'd have to become even more pliable if dinner went well tonight. What would filming for sixteen hours a day really look like? He imagined having to wait and do hundreds of re-takes until production was happy with the end result. He'd likely have to play into manufactured drama of some sort, for ratings of course, his life becoming one big fabricated roller coaster. Did he have the acting chops to pull it off? Or the patience?

He'd become accustomed to dictating his own schedule, for the most part. He'd never been very good at following the directions and mandates of others, except for Frances of course. Would he be selling his freedom if he signed on the dotted line of a TV contract?

Nathan's heart spasmed at the thought of that very probable reality. Was this what he really wanted?

When he thought about what he wanted, a certain blonde woman from his dreams floated across his inner screen. Immediately, he was transported back to where the dream left off, the tension in his body melting away. He imagined what it would be like to kiss her, to feel her perfect bow-shaped lips touch his, to taste her smile. Each time he was around her, it became increasingly difficult to stay true to his gentlemanly commitment.

But in his mind, Nathan knew it was best to avoid putting himself, and her, into that situation. Erin had her inn to look after, and he was a road warrior. Their worlds were so different, and she'd already expressed an aversion to travel. Besides, he enjoyed being a lone wolf, keeping his encounters with elegant does light and carefree until he boarded a plane and left them behind forever.

Nathan toweled off and got dressed. He'd never been the monogamous type. Actually, he'd never had a relationship to speak of beyond casual flings. He'd never been able to trust someone enough to let down his guard, always opting for self-preservation. Besides, the first woman who should have loved him unconditionally left him behind because of his faulty heart. He found it easier to keep his heart behind a cage, never taking the chance to let love in. However, as his thoughts wandered toward hunting down more fleeting relationships across the globe, his brow wrinkled. Something about that didn't feel right anymore.

But what other options were there? It wasn't like there were a ton of career choices for a globetrotting social influencer. He was getting tired of pursuing sponsorships on his own and knew TV was the most logical next step for him. And he had Frances to think about. He'd been helping her financially for years, despite her protests, and he knew she needed the money.

He took a deep breath. One thing was certain—he didn't need to have all the answers right then. He'd remain fluid and let the chips fall where they may during dinner.

ERIN HUSTLED into the dining room, carefully balancing a

plate of blueberry breakfast bread in one hand and butter and jam in the other. Fixing breakfast had proved to be a challenge that morning, having to maneuver around the industrial-sized fans she'd placed in the kitchen to help dry up the remaining moisture. On the plus side, she noticed everything appeared almost back to normal, and there wasn't any substantial damage to her flooring that would need serious repair. However, she made a mental note to call Hank Vargas, the handyman Brooke and Ted both recommended, just to double check the dishwasher was still functional and assess any water damage beyond what her eyes could see.

The Abernathys must have decided to sleep in, but her new guest, Lorna Frasier, sipped coffee and read a paperback with a Fabio look-alike on the cover at a dining table. She'd checked in late last night and planned to stay one more night.

"Could I interest you in a piece of breakfast bread, Mrs. Frasier?" Erin asked.

Lorna shook her head. "Coffee is fine this morning, thank you." She turned her attention back to her novel. "And you can call me Lorna," she added, not breaking attention from the page.

"Okay, Lorna. Let me know if you need anything else." Erin took the opportunity to return to the kitchen and dial the number for Hank. She left a message on his voicemail and returned to the dining room with fresh coffee. She refilled Lorna's cup. The guest thanked her without making eye contact. Erin didn't think Fabio was all that enthralling, but she could see how some women might think he was. Her type was more adventurous. Well-traveled. Named Nath—

"Just who I was looking for," Nathan said, entering the room and interrupting her thoughts.

"Oh?" Erin blushed. She looked at her hands holding the carafe. "Because I've got coffee?"

Nathan looked at her hands too. "Sure, I'll take some."

Erin filled a cup and handed it to Nathan, fingers lightly brushing his during the hand-off.

"I just got off the phone with my publicist. She told me one of the executives had a conflict come up and needs to move dinner to tonight instead of tomorrow. I'm hoping that won't be a problem and you'll still be able to accompany me." He grimaced, obviously anticipating the worst.

Erin paused. Before she could overthink it, the words, "Sure, that's fine. I'll make that work," flowed from her lips. Her eyebrows raised. Fluidity wasn't her normal M.O.

Nathan looked relieved. "Thanks, I really appreciate it. I don't know where dinner will be yet, but I should be back no later than—"

Erin's phone rang. "Hold that thought one second." She held up a finger. "This might be a handyman calling me back." She answered. It was the handyman confirming he could come by in about an hour to assess the damage. She agreed and they hung up. "Where were we?" she said, just as the phone for the inn rang. She rushed toward the desk phone. "Keep holding that thought."

"Hello, is this the Gilded Rose?" the caller asked.

"Yes, and this is Erin. How can I help?"

"I'm calling because my niece is getting married at Cheshire Moon next month, and I'm hoping you have room to accommodate some of the wedding party."

Erin could hardly contain the smile growing on her face. "Yes, let me check my date book. How many are in your party?"

The caller gave her more details as Erin checked her guestbook. She was pretty sure things were wide open, but then she paused. The calendar had filled up quite a bit while she and Nathan were at the winery. Apparently, Violet had booked several couples for the first two weeks in September, making a note that they'd all come from Nathan's social media posts with many smiley faces. Erin had a huge smile to match as she forced herself to stay present and take down more details from the caller. "Just curious, how'd you hear about us?"

"I spoke with a lovely woman…Cassandra, I think it was. She highly recommended your inn."

Erin beamed. "Great, we look forward to seeing you next month. The hyacinth and freesias will be blooming then in our garden, so be sure to plan on taking some photos here around your special day."

They said their goodbyes and hung up. Erin rushed back into the dining room, completely elated at the turning of the tide. "You won't believe what just happened."

"What? Who was that?"

"That was someone whose niece is getting married at Cheshire Moon and needed accommodations for fourteen people. I'll be fully booked that weekend. And I looked at the guestbook, and it appears Violet booked several couples yesterday who had phoned after seeing your social media posts. I can't believe it. Thank you so much." She practically leapt toward him, wrapping her arms around his neck to embrace him in a hug.

Nathan slowly placed a hand on the small of her back, pulling her into his embrace. A picture of Adam flashed in her mind's eye, and she started to pull away, but Nathan held her tighter. She looked up into his eyes and felt the undeniable heat building between them, his gaze penetrating her resolve. Her pulse raced as she licked her lips. His eyes dropped to her mouth. Before she could think, his lips were on hers.

She'd heard of men kissing with strong lips from an 80s movie. And while she'd experienced some really great kisses throughout her life, none of her previous kissers could be described as having strong lips. As Nathan pressed his lips to hers, she suddenly knew what that movie touted all those years ago. His lips were strong. She felt his kiss radiate through her entire body. Not just her lips, but her elbows, her stomach, even her kneecaps, which threatened to give out from under her.

His hands cupped her face, his fingers quickly traveling to comb through the blond strands near her temple. He pulled her head closer to his, deepening their kiss. Her mouth parted, inviting his tongue to meet hers. The taste of rich coffee enhanced the depth of the kiss, and the scent of his orange and ginseng cologne tickled her senses. Her hands ran across his muscular shoulders, feeling them flex under her delicate touch.

He was absolutely delicious.

Then, he pulled away, leaving Erin shellshocked. Before she completely got her bearings, she heard a guttural sound.

"Ahem, I could use more coffee over here if you're not too engrossed," Lorna said.

"Sorry," Nathan mumbled.

Lorna rolled her eyes, retreating back to the dining room.

"Well, I better get back to it," Erin said, resisting the magnetic pull to leap back into his arms. "You'll let me know about tonight?"

Nathan nodded. "As soon as I know, you will too. Looking forward to it." He was breathless, lust coating his voice. Clearly, she wasn't the only one feeling completely inconvenienced by the nature of her business.

"Me too," Erin stalled, staring into Nathan's eyes, unable to turn away. Lorna cleared her throat loudly again, and Erin had no choice but to break the spell. She picked up the carafe and walked to Lorna's table to refill her mug. When she looked up, Nathan was gone. "Sorry 'bout that."

"It's easy to get distracted by someone like him," Lorna said. "Have you been dating long?"

"Oh, we're not dating."

"Huh, could've fooled me." Lorna took a sip of her black coffee. "You two remind me of me and my Kip."

"Kip?"

"My late husband, God rest his soul." Lorna made a cross over her chest, looking up toward the ceiling. "He died from Lou Gehrig's. Still miss him."

"I'm so sorry." Erin placed a sympathetic hand on Lorna's shoulder, then pulled it back in fear of wrinkling her guest's perfectly pressed shirt. "How long ago, if you don't mind my asking?"

"Fifteen years. He used to look at me the way that young man looks at you, that's why I assumed—" Lorna motioned with her hand. "Sorry."

"It's okay," Erin said. "I sympathize with you, actually. Lost my husband a little over a year ago."

"But you're so young," Lorna said, confusion clouding her brow. "What . . .how?"

"Motorcycle crash."

"That's awful." She shook her head, pain and empathy visible in her eyes.

Erin had grown accustomed to most people going silent once they'd heard what ultimately took Adam's life. There wasn't much that could be said. Sometimes, she'd have people placate her with shallow apologies for her loss, obviously never having experienced a loss as great themselves. She appreciated the silence for once, knowing her guest truly understood the pain she had endured. However, she certainly didn't envy Lorna. She felt thankful in that moment that Adam was taken away swiftly. She couldn't imagine watching him wither away from the inside, his body unable to keep up with his still-sharp mind as it succumbed to a disease like

ALS. And it was apparent by looking at Lorna that kind of loss never got easier.

On the other hand, there was no sense in dwelling in the past. Brooke stressed to her the importance of moving forward, and Erin had started to do that. She was almost ready to try sleeping without the body pillow on the other side of the bed. She'd made some good strides lately. Although she felt like she'd taken a giant leap that morning into Nathan's arms, feeling his kiss lingering on her lips. Had she moved too quickly too soon? After all, he was leaving in a couple of days. What would happen then?

"You know, I think I might have some blueberry bread. You sure I can't offer you a piece?"

Lorna considered her offer. "Fine, twist my arm." She smiled.

Erin grabbed two pieces of bread and joined Lorna at her table. Lorna cut a piece off the corner with a fork, taking a bite. Her disposition changed, and Erin sensed Lorna's energy brighten.

"This is delicious," Lorna mumbled, taking another bite. A smile spread across her face. "It tastes like wildflowers in a meadow on a warm sunny day. I'm impressed."

"I've nicknamed it sunshine bread," Erin said.

"I need the recipe for this." She studied her plate.

"You'll have to get it from my friend Brooke. She's the one who made it. She owns Batter Up downtown. And good luck; she won't even tell *me* what her secret is."

"I'll add that to my stops today." Lorna pulled a small notepad from her purse and wrote down Brooke's address. Erin noticed there were a few indiscernible items on her to-do list and couldn't help wondering how Lorna intended to spend her one day in Mystic Beach.

"What else is on your agenda today?" Erin asked.

Lorna shrugged. "Just go with the flow, I guess. Usually,

Kip had a packed itinerary when we traveled, and I still haven't gotten used to not having someone dictate to me how to spend every moment of a vacation."

Erin took a bite, considering suggestions. "A lot of people like to check out the lighthouse down near Brannan Point."

"Kip loved lighthouses," Lorna volunteered. "I should do that."

"Good morning, beautiful," Mr. Abernathy sang as he and Mrs. Abernathy entered the dining room.

Erin stood to greet the Abernathys. They were wearing matching emerald polyester pants and plaid golf hats with a ball of fuzz on top. "How'd you sleep?"

"Not very well, in a good way." He winked.

"Harold, really," Mrs. Abermathy chided.

"What?" Harold played dumb.

Erin chuckled. "Let me set you two up over here." She guided them to a table near a bay window overlooking the garden. She filled their coffee mugs, emptying the last of the carafe. "I'll be back. I need to brew more coffee. Help yourselves to blueberry breakfast bread, eggs, and bacon whenever you're ready."

"You *must* have some of the bread," Lorna stressed. "It's divine."

The Abernathys were in their own world, fixing each other's coffee, trembling hands hovering over trembling hands as they stirred the other's cup.

Now that's love. She hoped one day she might find someone who would start a coffee ritual with her, insisting on fixing her cup before their own. She heard Lorna sigh as the Abernathys sipped their coffee after clinking their mugs together. She headed back toward the kitchen to brew more coffee, musing about the idea of finding her own Mr. Coffee.

*H*er lips still tingled.

Erin's pulse raced as Hank examined the kitchen. She braced herself for the worst, yet remained hopeful for the best. It didn't sound promising as he tinkered around with the dishwasher. As much as she struggled to stay present while the handyman assessed the damage, lust twirled like a tornado inside her. She couldn't stop thinking about Nathan and how his kiss blew her away. Since meeting him, she'd imagined more than once what it might feel like to kiss him, and her imagination paled in comparison to reality. She brought her fingertips to her lips to make sure they were still intact. *If he kissed like that, just think how well he'd do other things.* Erin blushed at the thought, a smile creeping across her face before she forced it away in the presence of her handyman.

"Well, Mrs. Pedersen, what do you want first, the good news or the bad news?"

"Good, No, wait. Bad." She took a deep breath. "Hit me with it, whichever."

He cracked a smile, revealing a gold crown. "Okay, the

good news is your flooring didn't sustain much water damage. None of the wood will need to be replaced, but we'll need to refinish it."

"Great." She exhaled. "What about the bad news?"

"Your dishwasher needs a replacement part. Because of the age of this machine, I'll need to custom order it, and it could take up to two weeks for it to come in." He grimaced. "Also, I can't get back to refinish the floors until next Tuesday. I'm booked solid."

"Okay, that's fine. I had a feeling that might be the case. What's the damage?"

"With both repairs we're looking at…" He paused, doing mental math. "Around twelve hundred dollars. All depends on the cost of that replacement part."

Erin had to keep her jaw from dropping. She sighed. "Okay, thanks Hank."

"It could have been much worse," he offered. "Your floors could have needed replacing. And hey, they don't make dishwashers like this one anymore." He tapped the metal door. "A lot of the new models are junk, frankly. You've got yourself a fine piece of machinery here that needs a little tune up, that's all."

"Thanks for the reassurance." Erin forced a thin smile.

"I'll go ahead and get the part ordered. I'll call you with an update on arrival and will see you Tuesday morning to refinish the floors. Sound good?" When Erin nodded, he said goodbye and headed toward another appointment.

Erin sat in a chair at the kitchen table. *Twelve hundred dollars?* That would put a nice dent in her savings. Thankfully, Ted would reimburse her at some point, but she still needed to front the cash. She knew handling repairs was par for the course in owning a business, but she'd expected there to be more in reserves and heavier traffic flow when she took the place over. It hadn't been much more than a money pit lately, and she rubbed her forehead, wondering what could possibly go wrong next.

Maybe she should consider putting the inn up for sale. She still wasn't sure she was cut out for it. If she were this disturbed over a minor repair, did she really have any business continuing down this path? Besides, how would she react if, no, *when*, the roof needed to be replaced or she needed to have the inn tented for termites? The idea made her skin crawl.

After all, there was a reason Erin stuck with finance. It was absolute. The numbers didn't lie. Everything was black and white. She could probably go back to San Francisco and get her old job back pretty easily. She'd slip right back into her old routine, feeling the comfort of receiving a steady paycheck for work she could do in her sleep. She'd be closer to Adam's memory, able to visit his resting place more frequently. And when she felt ready, she could dip a toe in the dating pool, likely seeing a software engineer who appreciated binary definitives too. How bad could that be?

Her mind wandered to Brooke and Violet. They'd quickly become like family to her in the time she'd been back in her hometown. Even the women she met last night at the book club felt more like sisters than acquaintances after one simple evening. How would she be able to tell them she'd decided to take the path of least resistance? Somehow, she felt if she returned to her old life, she'd be taking the easy way out and miss something truly special. Despite the discomfort she currently felt from being completely outside of her comfort zone, Erin knew she had to see it through. Even for a little while longer.

"Rooms are done." Violet entered the kitchen, holding a broom and a basket full of general cleaning supplies. She studied Erin. "You okay?"

Erin shook her head. "I will be. Eventually."

Violet put away the cleaning supplies and joined Erin at the table. "What's wrong? What can I do?"

Erin groaned. "You wouldn't happen to have an extra grand lying around?"

Violet grimaced. "The repairs?"

Erin nodded. "But the good news is he'll be able to refinish the floors next week, and Ted will reimburse me at some point."

Violet shrugged. "Could be worse."

"You're right," Erin said. "He could promise two weeks and it turns into two months instead." Erin forced a laugh.

"See? Bright side," Violet said. "Speaking of, did you see how many bookings we have from Nathan's post?"

Erin nodded. "And now we're completely booked for a wedding party the last weekend in September."

Violet shrieked. "Why didn't you lead with that?" She playfully slapped Erin's arm. "Here you are acting all depressed, and for what? That's great news!"

"I certainly hope so. We've gotta pull it off first," Erin said.

"You will. *We* will." She placed a reassuring hand on top of Erin's. "Hey, you should suggest they have Brooke make the wedding cake."

"You talkin' 'bout me in here?" Brooke entered through the back door.

"Erin got a reservation for an entire wedding party at the end of September." Violet beamed.

"Wow, congrats girl. And yes, I'd be honored to make their cake if they want." Brooke placed a hand over her heart.

"There's no one else I'd recommend," Erin said.

Brooke looked over her shoulder conspiratorially before pulling up a chair. "So, what's the latest with Nathan? Any news on where you're going tomorrow night?"

"Tonight," Erin corrected. She hoped her face didn't give

away any aftershocks from their earlier earth-shattering kiss. Besides, she was never the type to kiss and tell.

Brooke raised an eyebrow. "How're you handling the change?"

"I'm still in sticker shock over the repairs Hank quoted me, which has distracted me from the change." And that kiss.

"Wait, what's going on?" Violet looked confused.

"Our friend here has a date with Mr. Scott this evening," Brooke offered.

"It's not a date. It's a business meeting," Erin amended.

Violet playfully punched Erin again. "And you didn't tell me? Ugh, I'm so jealous. Who cares about the repairs? You're going out with Nathan."

"Yeah, but she's insisting it's not a date," Brooke said.

"Whatever," Violet said. "I've seen the way they look at each other."

Erin blushed. "I don't know what you're talking about."

Brooke laughed. "Have you decided what you're wearing to your *business meeting*?" She used air quotes around the last two words.

Erin shook her head. "I thought I had more time to plan."

"What about that sexy black halter dress you've got buried in the back of your closet?" Violet suggested.

"I'm not sure that's appropriate."

"For your non-date. Right." Violet smiled, rolling her eyes.

"No, that's more than appropriate," Brooke said. "Done. What else?" Before Erin could protest, Brooke countered, "You've got that purple shawl you can use to keep your shoulders warm. Besides, it's not supposed to be too cold tonight."

"How'd you know?" Erin wrinkled her brow.

"I know you just a little bit." Brooke held her fingers close together.

"For someone who is going out with Nathan Scott, you sure don't seem too enthused," Violet said. "What gives?"

Erin sighed. "I just—I don't know. Do you think it's too soon?"

"For what? Dinner?" Brooke said.

"A girl's gotta eat, right?" Violet said.

"She's right." Brooke pointed at Violet.

"I wonder if I'm disrespecting Adam's memory somehow." Erin looked up from the invisible piece of lint she'd picked off her shirt to see Violet and Brooke looking at her like she'd sprouted another head. "I guess I'm overthinking it."

"Probably. Unless you're feeling something a little more than business toward him." Violet gave her an impish smile, hoping Erin would dish more than she was.

"Just go with the flow tonight and stop thinking. It's not a marriage proposal, it's dinner," Brooke said.

The mention of a proposal made Erin's heart flutter. "I hope you're right."

So much for his resolve to not make a mess of things.

Nathan shook his head, packing up his belongings to head out of the breakout room after his panel discussion. While most people would say he nailed it, he knew better than to agree. He was distracted, having to ask the facilitator to repeat the question at least three times.

He couldn't stop thinking about that kiss. It was unlike anything he'd ever experienced. Sure, he'd had some great kisses with beautiful women throughout the globe, but this was different. He'd replayed it over and over in his mind from the moment she instinctively leapt into his arms from the sheer joy of booking the inn for an entire weekend. The faint smell of her coconut shampoo and green tea-scented skin. How naturally she fit in his arms. How he didn't want to let her go. How her lips tasted so sweet. The small whimper she made when he combed his fingers through her hair before deepening their kiss.

She was irresistible.

All he could think about was how and when he could kiss her again. Perhaps no one would interrupt for a coffee refill. What would happen then? He didn't think he was strong enough to hold back, wanting to explore all of her, every inch, hearing her whimper from his delicate touch.

And now he was supposed to take her to dinner. The dinner that would make or break his next career move. And keep his hands to himself.

What kind of torture was this? Normally, he wasn't so cruel to himself. But in his defense, it wasn't often a woman got under his skin. Who was he kidding? No woman had ever made him feel the way Erin did. She made his heart flutter. It terrified him.

Regardless of how he was feeling, he couldn't lose sight of his goal, especially with everything riding on this weekend. Aside from that, he'd be leaving in a couple of days, with or without a television contract. And definitely without Erin. It was the best for both of them. He'd only break her heart.

Although he felt like his would break when he imagined saying goodbye to her at the end of the weekend.

His phone rang, saving him from the painful imagery. It was Coco.

"How'd your panel go this afternoon?"

"It went as well as expected," he feigned.

"Great. I've got an update on dinner for you. It looks like you'll be meeting at Blowfish at 7:30 pm."

"Sounds good. Just enough time to go home and change and pick up my date." He squinted. *Home.* He'd never said that before about a place except for Seattle.

"Home, huh?" she teased.

Nathan cleared his throat. "Wherever I am is home at the moment. Occupational hazard."

"Okay, just don't get too comfortable. Word is they're planning to film the pilot in Kuala Lumpur and will want to move forward quickly to meet their aggressive production schedule."

"Understood." Nathan's heart twinged. He'd grown accustomed to uncomfortable feelings in his heart his whole life, but this pang was different. This was still everything he wanted, right?

"Okay, kid, let me know how things go tonight. I'm on pins and needles over here. And take it from me—stop and pick up some flowers for that beautiful woman of yours."

Nathan smiled. "Okay, Coco, but she's not my woman. She's just my date."

"For now."

Nathan chuckled. "Talk to you later." They hung up. He grabbed his leather messenger bag and left the breakout room. He ran into Paul outside the room. He had an arm around Heather and Melissa, who was laughing hysterically at something Paul must have said.

"Good job, mate." Paul patted Nathan on the shoulder. "Let's get you a celebratory beer."

"Thanks, but afraid I'll have to stop you there. I've got other plans tonight."

"Oh, come on," Melissa said. "I don't bite."

"I do," Heather said.

Paul nodded. "I can attest to that." Heather cackled.

Nathan caught himself before his face contorted too much in disgust. "Next time, but please have one for me." He walked away before they tried to convince him otherwise.

He couldn't help thinking that, under different circumstances, he would have jumped at the opportunity to have a wingman like Paul for a weekend like this. Having a partner in crime increased the odds of finding a good time, fleeting as it might be. Seeing his old behavior reflected back to him now seemed cheap, superficial, and downright boring. He shuddered in embarrassment at what he once thought constituted a good time.

What sounded like an even better time to him now was sitting in the garden at The Gilded Rose with Erin, a bottle of pinot grigio to share while they looked at the stars. He'd light a fire in a fire pit and would pull her close to keep her warm in the chilly twilight breeze off the ocean. His skin would fire to life feeling her body next to his, and he'd kiss her senseless, touching every curve…

He shook his head. He needed to keep his attention on the task at hand, which was securing the offer from the executives tonight. He felt confident the offer would be his, especially after talking to Coco. And with Erin on his arm. She was definitely his secret weapon.

But he couldn't help feeling she was also his kryptonite.

*N*athan perched on a bench in the garden and waited for Erin, twirling a single red rose in his fingers. He tried to distract his mind as it ricocheted through a multitude of possible outcomes for the evening by watching the sun descend, mesmerized by the pink and purple ribbons twirling through the sky as twilight took over Mystic Beach. Stars blinked to life, preparing to shine brightly in the impending darkness. He took deep breaths, not allowing his nerves to get the best of him. Although he wasn't sure which was more nerve-racking: his date or meeting with the executives.

"I'm ready," Erin said.

Nathan stood, turning to see Erin's silhouette in the French door frame.

Oh, dear God.

His heart caught in his throat. He'd never seen a woman look more beautiful. Erin wore a black halter dress with her hair swept up in a clip, accentuating her elegant neckline. He tried hard to resist burying his face in her neck, placing a trail of kisses down to her delicate collarbone. A purple sash covered her shoulders, although he could think of better ways to keep her warm in the evening breeze. Her simple heels brought her a little closer to his eye line, and he swallowed hard. "You look…"

"Is this okay?" Erin looked down at her dress. "If it's too much or not enough, I can—"

"You're perfect." He held her gaze, feeling electricity flicker between them. She was trouble in the best way possible, and he considered taking her up to his room and blowing off dinner altogether. But he knew he couldn't do that. He'd worked so hard to get to this point and needed to keep his eye on the prize. Although he wondered what the true prize was with her already by his side. "This is for you." He handed her the rose.

Erin blushed. "Thank you." She smiled and took the rose from his hand, their fingers grazing slightly. She brought the flower to her nose, breathing deeply. "It's beautiful."

Nathan nodded, unable to tear his gaze away from the delicate woman before him. He'd never envied a flower so much, wishing he were that close to her beautiful lips and able to taste her sweetness with a kiss. "Shall we?" He held out his arm for her to grab.

"We shall," Erin said, looping her arm in his as they made their way through the garden toward his car. Having Erin on his arm felt natural, like she'd finally made her way home. He thought about his slip of calling this place home earlier when he was on the phone with Coco. There was no denying it; he could get used to this. Used to spending time with her. He didn't want it to end.

"Nervous?" she asked.

"Slightly. But I'm feeling better since I'm bringing my secret weapon." He winked.

She chuckled. "Something tells me this is a formality and you've already got it in the bag."

"I appreciate the vote of confidence." He temporarily let go of her arm to open the passenger door of his car. "Madam," he said, holding out his hand to help her in.

"Good sir." She laughed and took his hand. "We're medieval now, huh?" They both smiled. Once she was settled, he closed the door and walked around the car to get in the driver's seat. She surprised him by reaching across and opening his door for him.

He smiled and thanked her, starting the car. They drove in silence as he wound through hills before accelerating onto the freeway toward San Francisco. She crossed her legs, bringing his attention to the silky smooth skin on her thigh. He imagined lifting her dress a little higher, touching her—

"Look out!"

He swerved, barely missing a guardrail on the right. *Dude, get it together.* He shook his head. "Sorry 'bout that." He felt like an idiot.

"Twice in one week. Do you have a death wish?" she teased.

He let out a nervous chuckle. "Unfamiliar roads in the dark, I guess." And his beautiful co-pilot didn't help. *Focus.*

"I'm sure there's a clause in your pending contract that you must be alive for it to be awarded." A smile tugged at her lips.

He shrugged. "My publicist could probably argue that and win."

She laughed. "Sounds like she's good at her job."

"She's the best." He took an exit for another freeway. "Distract me. Tell me something about you that no one knows."

Erin crossed her arms. "Like what?"

"I don't know, anything."

Erin paused. "I can't whistle."

Nathan chuckled. "Really? Of all things that make up who Erin is, you tell me you can't whistle?"

Erin smiled. "I don't know. I cracked under the pressure."

He laughed. "Wow, it's a good thing I'm finding this out now."

"You needed a whistler for tonight?"

"Not that I know of. But there might be rapid fire questions. Quick, I'm an executive. Why should we award the show to Nathan? Aaaand...go."

"Umm..." Erin stammered, playing with the hem on her dress.

"Come on, time is money. I'm not buying it." He tapped his wrist where a watch would be.

"Because he's cute?" Erin blushed. "I mean, he would look good on camera."

"You think so?" Nathan grinned.

"Wait, shouldn't you be answering that question? I think you reversed our roles."

"I was hoping to crowdsource my answer from you. I think I'll lead with that."

"Very funny." She playfully slapped his shoulder as they both laughed.

Nathan turned into the parking lot of Blowfish, an upscale sushi restaurant overlooking San Francisco Bay. He pulled up to the valet, who took his keys to park the car. He placed a hand on the small of Erin's back and propelled her toward the entrance. Her silky dress felt cool to his touch, and now that he was no longer behind the wheel, he allowed his mind to wonder about her smooth skin underneath.

Erin stopped, turning to him. "Okay, take a deep breath. You got this." She placed a supportive hand on his shoulder.

Nathan looked into her green eyes, which sparkled in the string lights wrapped around a nearby tree. He wasn't sure who was more nervous: him or her. He certainly felt like he couldn't fail with her support. Something told him he didn't want to lose it, either. It wasn't every day a woman like Erin came waltzing into his life. There she was, encouraging him before the opportunity of a lifetime, and they barely knew each other. Yet there was something about her that was very familiar, like he'd known her for years. He couldn't explain it, and in no way was it rational, but he realized at that moment that if he allowed himself to, he could fall for this woman. Hard.

Had he already?

"Nathan?"

He took her hand, swallowing hard. "I want to say thank you for coming with me tonight. It means a lot."

"My pleasure." She held his hand tighter, giving it a gentle squeeze. "Now let's go win you that contract."

Keeping her hand in his, he went inside. The restaurant was decorated in rich mahogany woven through concrete and steel, giving it a modern and industrial flare. A large fish tank with many vibrant colored fish kept the front desk company, and the hostess notified them the rest of their party was already there. She led them toward a table near a window overlooking the bay, twinkling lights reflecting in the placid water. Two couples smiled as they approached, one man with chestnut brown hair the first to stand.

"Nathan? Jeff Fisher." His handshake was bone crushing firm. "Thanks for making tonight work." The smile reached his coffee-brown eyes.

"Yes, Jeff had something come up and needs to meet with Dale Ruiz tomorrow in Los Angeles to discuss this project. Simon Wallace. Pleasure." He shook Nathan's hand, sizing him up, which was hard to do considering Nathan towered over him by at least five inches.

"Who do we have here?" Jeff asked, eyeing Erin.

"I'm Erin. Nice to meet everyone." She gave an awkward but cute wave to everyone at the table, making eye contact with no one in particular.

"Ah, excellent. He brought someone to keep us company," Jeff's wife said. "You're already off to a good start. I'm Babs, and this is Lisa." Lisa gave a curt nod, her dangly gold earrings jingling against her shoulders.

"Shall we order? I'm rather peckish," Simon said, the pendant light reflecting off his receding hairline.

"When are you ever not, dear?" Lisa joked, playfully pushing his shoulder.

"You'll probably be peckish again in an hour after sushi." Jeff laughed loudly at his own joke. Babs joined in, her laughter more like a bird compared to Jeff's booming timbre.

Sensing he wasn't the only one who needed to relax, Nathan glanced at the sake menu, taking the liberty of ordering two bottles for the table. Simon snuck in an order of wagyu carpaccio. And yellowtail.

"And spring rolls. Don't forget shrimp spring rolls," Lisa called over her shoulder to the waiter, who quickly took down the order.

As they made small talk about TravelCon, Nathan reached for Erin's hand under the table, giving it a reassuring squeeze. He wanted to make sure she didn't feel excluded, and she glanced in his direction and smiled before Babs reached over to touch Erin's shawl, complimenting her ensemble. Nathan watched from the corner of his eye how Babs and Lisa quickly took to her, seeing firsthand how well Erin fit into his world. But he reminded himself she'd never consider living out of a suitcase, and he certainly wasn't ready to settle down. Regardless, he appreciated it for what it was in the moment.

Jeff commended Nathan on his participation as a panelist, drawing his full attention. "I snuck in toward the end, but I got to see you in action and under pressure. I have to admit —I was impressed. There were some tough questions thrown your way, and you handled them like a pro."

Erin reached over and squeezed Nathan's arm. He almost forgot what Jeff had just said, enchanted by Erin's smile. "Thank you, sir. I try to be prepared as much as possible, but I've learned in my time on the road to be fluid and adaptable since things change on a dime."

"Like your twenty-five-hour layover in Mumbai?" Lisa raised sake to her lips with a hand adorned by rings on every finger.

"Yes, my wife is obviously a fan of yours, which I'm not sure if that's an advantage or not," Simon teased.

"I think it's safe to say all women are fans of Nathan." Babs smiled slyly. Nathan blushed; he'd always had a way with redheads. "Don't you get jealous?" She looked at Erin.

Erin shrugged. "Nathan and I have an understanding. I trust him."

Damn. Her response was perfect. He couldn't have planned it better if he tried, and he placed his hand delicately behind her head, pulling her closer as he lightly brushed his lips across her forehead. When he pulled back, she looked deeply into his eyes, and her mouth parted before she bit her bottom lip. He wished they were alone so he could kiss her elsewhere.

"Whew, you two." Lisa fanned herself.

Babs elbowed Jeff. "How come you never kiss my forehead?"

Simon laughed nervously. "Nathan, you're making us look bad."

Their appetizers arrived, and conversation flowed effortlessly as they all sampled bites of everything. Jeff ordered more sashimi and a few hand rolls for the table, and Nathan barely registered what they'd eaten. He struggled to take his attention from Erin, thinking about how much he'd like to devour her.

"I have to address the elephant in the room," Simon said.

"We know about your heart. Lisa showed us a post from one of your social media profiles, and it wasn't hard to put two and two together."

Nathan's whole body stiffened. He didn't want Erin to find out this way about his heart, and he stole a quick glance in her direction to gauge her reaction. She appeared unfazed, which made him even more nervous. He was planning to tell her when the timing felt right but hadn't gotten around to it yet. Besides, they'd only known each other for a few days, and it's not like the subject of heart transplants comes up in everyday conversation. But he'd be lying if he said he wasn't kicking himself for finding a way to bring it up somehow.

"So, you're good to commit to a heavy travel schedule and the demands required for filming sometimes sixteen hours a day, right?" Jeff asked.

Nathan shifted uncomfortably. "Yeah, I've never been better since my heart transplant. If you need to speak with my surgeon or doctor or whomever, I can arrange that. But I'm a new man since the surgery, and I'm committed to whatever is necessary to get the job done."

Simon and Jeff looked at each other, and Simon gave a barely noticeable nod. "Good."

Something told Nathan a decision had been made right then and there. This was everything he'd ever hoped for and had been working toward his entire life. Now, it seemed like it was his for the taking. He looked at Erin, who smiled warmly at him before turning back to Lisa and Babs as they gossiped about the royal baby or whatever the latest tabloids touted. Erin had certainly come to mean more to him than just a casual date or a weekend fling, the realization of which made his second-chance heart leap into his throat.

Why was it now, of all times, that his heart chose to dive off a cliff? The last thing he had time for was building a relationship. Not that he even really knew what that took, since most of the time, he was on a plane again before things got too messy. Case in point—this weekend was unfolding like many others he'd experienced in far off places. He'd woo a beautiful woman, share a nice meal, perhaps share her bed, and then leave. But there was no denying the way he felt about Erin was different. Part of him struggled with the idea of leaving her in less than forty-eight hours. In fact, between the ideas of leaving Erin and his feelings for her, he wasn't sure which terrified him more.

But the real question in his mind was if she was feeling the same way about him.

THAT SEEMED TO GO WELL. *Really* well.

Everything that evening felt natural, from their silly banter in the car to the way Nathan kissed her forehead at dinner. It felt like they'd been a couple for years, with everything moving seamlessly, like clockwork. She hadn't felt so in sync with anyone except Adam and wasn't sure she'd ever feel that way again. But there she was, on the edge of something, preparing to fall.

However, she couldn't help questioning the ease of everything. The last time she'd experienced feelings like this, she'd ended up broken hearted, but that was an unfair comparison. Besides, it wasn't like anyone could have predicted Adam's early departure. Although, with Nathan about to leave in less than two days, she realized she wasn't ready for him to go either.

So many wise lovers over the ages proclaimed to love with total abandon. She had in the past and was starting to believe she could again, especially with how Nathan made her feel. The last thing she expected when Nathan showed up was to open her heart to a man again, especially one who, on paper, was all wrong for her. Their lifestyles couldn't be more different, although she was mostly comfortable getting a taste of what his world was like that evening. Yes, it all felt awkward at first, but her mind eased quickly, allowing her to have a good time. Was this all there was to it in his circle? If so, she *might* be able to get used to it. She wondered if Nathan were feeling the same way, but his silence on their drive home from Blowfish made her mind a little batty.

Were they already at the point of being comfortable in silence? Or did they both sense what would naturally happen next?

Her pulse raced. Of course, she'd thought about kissing him again. In fact, she couldn't stop thinking about how his lips felt against hers. The heat between them. The way he'd tenderly cupped her face. She thought he was going to kiss her again when they stopped in front of the restaurant before dinner, but he didn't. And when he tenderly kissed her forehead in the restaurant, it was one of the sweetest, gentlest gestures she'd ever experienced. She felt a yearning, a hunger, growing inside of her.

"Thank you for everything tonight," Nathan said, breaking their silence. He reached over to hold her hand as they drove, rubbing his thumb over her palm. She felt sparks travel throughout her body with every caress, the tender touch practically torture. She craved his touch throughout her entire body. She wanted more of him. All of him.

"I want to show you something." They'd just passed over the Golden Gate Bridge, and Nathan took an unexpected exit.

"Where are you going?" Erin asked.

"You'll see."

The unspoken promise in his tone made her pulse race. She couldn't tell which feeling was stronger, curiosity or desire, as he took an offbeat road leading down toward the shoreline. Gravel crunched under the wheels as he parked the car in a small, dimly-lit lot. He turned the engine off and faced her. "You okay to do a little walking in those shoes?"

"What are we doing?"

"You said you trusted me, right?"

Erin paused. "Y-yes." Was that still true? She felt in her bones that whatever happened next would change everything. Exactly what or how, she was unsure, but she knew if she stepped out of the car and went wherever Nathan was taking her, it would signify an end and a beginning. Was she ready to start a new chapter, whatever that may be? Was she officially closing the book on her old life?

For better or worse, they both got out of the car. Erin shuddered from what she told herself was the evening breeze.

"I don't think that wrap is going to cut it." Nathan quickly removed his jacket, his muscles flexing under the perfectly pressed Oxford. As he wrapped it around her shoulders, she felt the warmth from the heat from his body. The faint scent of his signature orange and ginseng cologne on the collar made her knees threaten to buckle.

He held out his hand. "Shall we?"

Erin hesitated, suffering from sensory overload. "Okay." Reticent, she placed her hand in his and he led her down a rocky path toward the shoreline. With every step, nerves fired through her body, while on the outside, she hoped she appeared cool and composed. They reached the shoreline and paused, looking up at the lights from the bridge, the low hum of traffic driving from one end to the next. The moon reflected off the bay, casting a warm glow on their dark figures.

"This is one of my favorite places in San Francisco." He pulled her into his embrace. "I wanted to share it with you."

"I can see why. This is beautiful." She'd never seen the city from this vantage point. The normal hustle and bustle seemed to move in slow motion. Or was it the close proximity to Nathan that made time feel like it was standing still?

He turned toward her. "I have to be honest with you about something." He took a deep breath. "I've been all over the world and have seen amazing places and met so many interesting people. San Francisco is one of my favorite cities in the entire world, but this time, it's different. More special. The difference has been you." He cupped her face in his palm. "You're an amazing woman, Erin, and I don't know what's going to happen, but I'm glad we've met."

Her skin electrified from his touch. She parted her lips, biting the bottom one as she gazed in his eyes. He leaned in, gently brushing her lips with his. Her spine tingled as he deepened the kiss, goosebumps canvassing her body. Their tongues danced slowly, finding a rhythm all their own as she pressed her body against his. Nothing else existed in the moment except his kiss, his touch, his tenderness.

He broke the spell, pulling back to look in her eyes. He brushed a loose strand of hair from her cheek, pushing it behind her ear. She shuddered, feeling on the brink of explosion from the heat between them. Succumbing to lust, she reached up and pulled his face closer to hers until their lips touched again. She wrapped her hands around his neck, and he gently pulled her closer to his body as their kiss ignited something that had been dormant in her for so long.

Erin knew it didn't make sense, but it was what she wanted. For however long it would last. Did it ever have to end? Nathan made her feel safe. Everything felt so right with him. Maybe she could give traveling a try. Perhaps she'd just had bad experiences before whenever she'd traveled, but it couldn't all be bad. It'd be fun with a globetrotter like Nathan taking the lead, whisking her off to different parts of the world. Undoubtedly, the man traveled in style, and she could too. They could explore the world together.

"I can't imagine saying goodbye to you," Nathan said, breathlessly breaking the spell between them. He nuzzled her neck, placing light kisses along her collarbone.

"Maybe you don't have to," she said without a thought.

He stopped kissing her, meeting her gaze. "What?"

She played with a button on his shirt, afraid she might lose her nerve. "I don't know. Maybe I could go with you… wherever you're going."

"What about the inn?" He took her hand, stopping her from fidgeting.

Temporarily speechless from his intense gaze, she swallowed hard and forced the words out. "Well, I've actually been thinking about selling the inn."

Nathan paused, processing what she'd just said. "You're not serious, are you?" His expression revealed nothing. His poker face was better than hers.

"Should I be?"

He broke contact from her, taking a step back. "You can't just uproot your life for me, Erin."

Stunned and confused, she opened her mouth and shut it, unsure of what to say.

"What about Nancy?" he asked.

"What about her?"

"She trusted you with the Rose," he said. "I know how much that means to you."

"So—" she stammered. "Well, then what the hell did you mean by you can't say goodbye to me?" Now Nathan appeared to be at a loss for words. "Do you plan to stop traveling? It's obvious you're going to get the contract for the show. What then?"

"I—I don't know." He ran a hand through his hair, parts of it sticking up in jagged points. She couldn't help thinking what he'd said was a line. A come-on to get into her pants. Was that his plan all along? Was she just another conquest to him, a notch on the bedpost? She felt sick and wrapped her arms protectively around her body. The scent of cologne wafted from his jacket toward her, fueling her anger. She tore off the jacket, forcing it back into his hands.

"Kendall was right; you *are* a player."

His jaw dropped, shock spreading across his face. "What are you—"

A bright light shined into their faces, stopping both of them in their tracks. A security guard, looking very perturbed, was on the other end of the light. Clearly, they had disturbed the peace. "You two need to leave," he said.

"Sorry, sir," Nathan said, waving a hand. "We'll get out of your way." He held out his hand for Erin to take, but she refused it, instead choosing to fumble her way up the rocky path toward the car in her poor choice of footwear alone.

*N*athan rolled over, defeated after a restless night. He'd spent countless hours wrestling with his mind, replaying his conversation along the shoreline with Erin as he thrashed in frustration under the covers. Of course, he had to choose that moment to stick his foot in his mouth.

The whole evening was perfect. Everything executed flawlessly. They'd bantered on the drive to the restaurant, and Erin proved she was certainly his secret weapon. And while Jeff and Simon seemed impressed by what Nathan had to offer, he was most impressed by Erin. She'd blown him away with her poise and authenticity under pressure. It felt totally natural to have her by his side, and his mind began to wander toward the idea of keeping her there more permanently.

And that's where things took a wrong turn.

He wasn't the monogamous type. His lifestyle wasn't conducive to anything more than a weekend fling every once in a while. Why on Earth he'd said it would be hard to say goodbye to her was beyond him. Yes, it was the honest to

God truth, but it didn't change the fact that she'd never be comfortable on the road, nor was he ready to permanently unpack his suitcase. So, when she casually mentioned the idea of selling the inn, he freaked. He couldn't take the pressure of having someone as special as Erin give up everything for him. Besides, he wasn't in a position to promise anything, and with her giving up everything, immensely high unspoken expectations would be tied to that sacrifice.

But then again, the idea of saying goodbye to her for good made his heart pang with emptiness, afraid he'd never be able to fully fill the void created by her absence. After experiencing the last few days with her, he'd felt a stirring in his heart that could only be summed up as falling. At least, based on what he knew from hearing others' experiences, and sappy made-for-TV movies. Life obviously had a sick sense of humor.

What the hell was wrong with him that he couldn't just let go and let her in?

Nathan's phone rang, and he answered before it rolled to voicemail. It was Coco.

"You did it, kid," she said. "It's in the bag. I'm looking at an email indicating a contract is coming. Congratulations!"

"Glad to hear."

Coco paused. "Are you sure? You don't sound too enthused."

"Sorry, it's still early," Nathan said, brushing it off. He felt mixed emotions hearing confirmation of what he'd expected when they left dinner last night. He should be happy, thrilled, to hear he'd be awarded the contract. But instead, his heart sank deeper. He felt like an imposter in his own being. It was a cruel joke. He couldn't imagine saying goodbye to Erin but couldn't accept her in his life more permanently. Regardless, he had no choice, so he better suck it up.

"Anywho," Coco continued, "I should have something a

little more formal by this afternoon, but I wanted to call and say congratulations. It seems having what's-her-name on your arm last night really helped seal the deal."

"Erin. Her name is Erin."

"Right. Erin. You should thank her. This is going to open many more doors for you. Speaking of that, a rep from Hyatt reached out to me asking if you were available to do a sponsorship spot next week in Jamaica."

Nathan sat on the edge of the bed to get his bearings. Everything was happening so quickly. Was this still what he wanted?

"Hellooo?"

"Sorry, yes. I'm available to do that."

"Great, I'll let them know and will have them book your travel."

Nathan swallowed hard. "Sounds good."

"And Nathan?"

"Hmm?"

"Good job. Frances is going to be so proud of you, as am I."

"Thanks." They hung up, and Nathan studied the wallpaper pattern, feeling a pit of dread. He knew going into the meeting that this was the expected outcome. So, why did he now feel like he was failing? By anyone's account, he was killing it, and Coco was right. Being on television was going to open so many doors for him in the future that his head spun just thinking about it.

But the last few days had been special. He felt different being in Mystic Beach. This place, the people, the food. It was pure magic. And the one wielding the magic wand had been Erin. Undeniably, in the last few days she'd cast her spell on him.

He felt a change, a shift between them ever since their first kiss and felt the same magnetic pull when they kissed again last night. But then he'd gone and put his foot in his mouth, quickly turning a wonderful evening into a disaster. Even if he could find the right words to make amends with her, what was the point? He'd be in Jamaica next week, Kuala Lumpur shortly after that, and maybe he'd squeeze in a visit to Seattle to celebrate with Frances. He never had time for matters of the heart in the past, and it appeared this time was no different.

He needed to do what he always did. Walk away. Withdraw. That was the best thing for both of them. But something fought hard within him, knowing that option was no longer possible. This time, he'd choose to defy logic. This time, he might just follow his heart.

WELL, things had gone from great to terrible in no time flat.

Erin wouldn't have predicted feeling so turned on and repulsed by the same man in less than a five-minute span. After a restless night's sleep, she no longer felt repulsed, but her heart ached. After replaying the evening over in her mind multiple times, she couldn't understand where things went off the rails.

They'd had a great time at dinner. Everything felt so natural between them. She'd allowed herself to picture what it might be like to date again. To date Nathan. The visions in her mind certainly didn't match reality when it came crashing down on her.

It had been so long since she'd felt any attraction, let alone a craving, for a man. She'd started to wonder if she would ever feel the pangs of desire for someone ever again. But spending the last couple of days with Nathan had sparked a part of her to life again she'd feared had died along with Adam. She felt desire and desired when they were together. As if they were stuck in a storybook, he'd brought her back to life with a simple kiss.

But nothing about the kiss last night was simple. Erin suspected her feelings weren't one-sided, but when Nathan freaked out after she hinted about a very real possibility of them having a future, it confused the hell out of her. Perhaps she'd read him all wrong.

Erin double-checked to be sure she was using the right type of soap before she closed the top lid on her washer, heading toward the dining room to clean up after breakfast. She cleared away dishes and wiped down tables, bringing everything back to the kitchen to soak in the sink.

She shook her head in embarrassment for calling him a player. She didn't mean it, and deep down, she knew it wasn't true. All signs pointed to Nathan being a genuinely nice man. He let creepy Ted believe he was Erin's boyfriend. He'd also helped give her the confidence boost she needed to forge her first partnership with Cheshire Moon, and she couldn't forget how he literally rolled up his sleeves and helped her clean up a soapy mess in her kitchen. He tenderly kissed her forehead. It's not everyday someone comes along who would do so many wonderful things with nothing much to gain in return.

One thing was certain—he was acting confused. But in his defense, did she know what she wanted either? Besides, in the light of morning, she couldn't help thinking about Adam. Sometimes, her heart still ached for him. He'd left a hole in her heart when he died, and she couldn't imagine anyone ever filling that void for her again.

Until Nathan.

Erin still struggled with the thought that she was betraying Adam's memory as she flirted with the idea of being with someone else. She knew if Adam could see her now, he'd want her to move on. It wasn't healthy to hold onto a memory, no matter how sweet. But that also didn't make it any easier to officially leave the past behind. She felt if she continued to open her heart to Nathan, she'd be closing the chapter of her life with Adam. Despite the feelings she'd experienced in the last few days, she wasn't sure she was ready to officially say goodbye.

She looked at the dishwasher, empty and lifeless, as she scrubbed dishes and put them in a drying rack. Maybe it was best she'd had an emotional outburst and said what she did. Perhaps it was the ice bath she needed to cool the fire burning in her for Nathan. Because if she were thinking rationally, there was no way she could get involved with someone like him. He'd be off to another corner of the world in another day or two, and she'd likely never see him again unless it was on her television screen. Their lives were far too different to make anything work.

"Grabbed the mail." Violet set the stack on the kitchen table.

Erin smiled. Right on top was a postcard from Hong Kong, which had to be from Kyle. She admired the picturesque scene of gondolas overlooking the bustling city below on a misty morning. He'd included a simple message: Thinking of you. Promise to call soon. Love, Kyle. She and Kyle didn't have a typical sibling relationship growing up. He never pulled her pigtails or listened in on her phone conversations with her best friend as they dissected teenage boy behavior. Instead, he'd always been a protector, standing up for her whenever she faced adversity. So, it was no surprise to her when he signed up to serve and protect the country.

She hadn't seen much of her brother since their mother's battle with cancer. He was able to take a brief leave from active duty, assisting with care and wrapping up affairs once her battle was lost. Erin and Kyle had made a tremendous team, working in tandem to make the tough decisions necessary when their father was too bereaved to function. It solidified their familial bond but also took their friendship to a higher level, with each being a dependable ally to the other. She admired his courage and hoped that once he retired from the service, he'd consider making Mystic Beach his home. Or wherever she ended up. She still needed to figure out what she truly wanted.

Erin didn't hesitate to put the postcard on her fridge, held up by a magnet he'd sent her from Beirut. She sifted through the rest of the stack, discarding irrelevant paper and card stock advertisements until she came across a letter from a law office in Chicago. How odd. She didn't know anyone in Chicago. Why would she be receiving a letter from a law office there? She ripped the side of the envelope, curious about the contents.

She unfolded a simple one-page letter and scanned it. It appeared someone was interested in buying The Gilded Rose. She felt her stance waiver, re-reading the letter again, with the generous figure with multiple zeroes at the end. Was this for real?

Part of her wasn't sure she was up for managing the inn long-term, and here the Universe had delivered her a way out in a cream-colored envelope. But Nancy had trusted her life's work to Erin, and if she took this easy way out, what would happen to her aunt's legacy? Where would Erin even go?

"What is it?" Violet eyed her cautiously.

Erin could only imagine what her expression must look like as she'd read that letter. "Nothing." She quickly folded the page, placing it under the rest of the stack. Despite the fact that Violet likely wouldn't be staying on to help for much longer, Erin didn't want her to be alarmed at the possibility of losing her temporary job.

Was she actually considering the offer?

Violet raised an eyebrow. "You sure?"

"Yeah, it's fine," Erin lied, waving her off. She looked at the rest of the pile, and a thick envelope caught her attention. She picked it up, a wrinkle forming above her forehead when she noticed it was from the transplant department at a hospital in Seattle. As she ran her fingers over it, she registered another envelope inside, like a Russian doll.

What was this—bizzaro mail day? Who would send her a letter in a letter from Seattle?

Realization hit her, knocking the wind right out of her lungs. It couldn't be, could it?

Erin barely heard Violet say she'd get started on the rooms. She plopped into a nearby chair to open the letter. She ripped open the envelope, revealing the second letter inside. Her fingertips traced the words Donate Life Network written on the outside of the light blue envelope. Whoever wrote it used force with their pen. The words felt like a new form of braille under her fingertips. She tore the second envelope, unfolding the letter to reveal the words she'd already anticipated reading. Words like *gratitude* and *a second chance at life*, and *no words could ever adequately express* floated in front of her eyes.

The rest of the words were lost to her in the moment, carried away in a sea of tears. She clutched the letter to her chest, allowing the tears to fall down her face without wiping them away. She needed this release more than she'd realized and didn't fight it. Erin's heart ached for her lost love as she read the letter. It transported her back to the accident and the moment she had to make the hardest decision of her life.

She didn't have Kyle there to lean on when she told the doctors to pull the plug. She'd done it alone. It was the loneliest she'd ever felt, hearing the machines lull to a stop, the rhythmic beeping slowly turning into a straight, steady line of lifelessness. She didn't wish that experience on anyone.

But knowing a part of Adam gave life to someone else who desperately needed it comforted her somehow. Part of him lived on. His heart touched someone else's life in ways she'd never fully understand. It made the pain she'd endured worth it on some level, bringing meaning to the incomprehensible agony of losing her husband.

Despite knowing his life saved another, she wished he were still alive. She didn't care if that made her selfish. But there was no changing the past, and she knew Adam would be happy to know his early departure wasn't made in vain. She imagined him looking down from Heaven, smiling at the new host for his heart as he lived fully and with total abandon for the first time in his life. There was a lot of beauty in the orchestration when she paused and viewed it objectively.

She wiped the tears from her face and clutched the letter to her chest. Adam wouldn't want her to wallow in pain. He'd want her to find happiness in his legacy being carried on through someone else. She'd have to find comfort in that somehow, and when she was done feeling selfish, she did.

13

———————————————

*A*fter attending the wrap-up events for TravelCon, Nathan pulled around to the side of The Gilded Rose and parked his rental car. He'd hoped the drive back would provide more clarity on what his next steps should be, but he came up short. He'd spent the whole drive feeling torn in two. Part of him felt ecstatic after hearing from Coco he'd be receiving paperwork from the network to solidify his start in television. However, he knew not to get too excited until he saw the official offer in writing. He'd learned the hard way that it wasn't a done deal until contracts were signed by both parties. Once it was inked, he'd have a true cause for celebration.

The other part of him dreaded the conversation he needed to have with Erin. Normally, at this point in a brief relationship, he'd be on a plane before having to endure any form of confrontation. After last night, he'd be lying if he said he didn't think about just letting things go. He considered letting her think he was a player, walking away, and never looking back. But he knew that would be the easy way out, and he just couldn't do it. He couldn't continue to run anymore. He couldn't bear the thought of leaving her on bad terms.

He knew allowing himself to accept and validate how she'd made him feel in the last few days would do nothing but create more heartache for both of them. Logically, he couldn't—shouldn't—allow himself to open his heart to this woman any more than he already had. He'd be leaving for Jamaica shortly and likely Kuala Lumpur after that. However, this time was different. No amount of distance between them would help him forget her smile, her soft skin, and the way her lips felt against his. He knew his heart would no longer allow him to deny the truth: he was falling for her.

The sun slowly crept toward the horizon for its daily descent, and Nathan locked his car and then walked toward the garden to take in one more sunset in Mystic Beach. He knew better than to try rehearsing a conversation, but his mind frantically attempted to construct the best way to express his jumbled mess of thoughts and feelings anyway. As he rounded the corner and placed a hand on the white picket gate, he heard a faint sniffle. Erin sat on a white bench looking toward the horizon with a balled-up tissue in her hand. She was oblivious to his presence, her shoulders quivering as she tried her best to control her emotions. Was he to blame for her emotional state? He felt sick to his stomach at the thought of causing her so much pain.

He must have made a noise because Erin quickly wiped her cheeks when she saw him.

"You okay?" He walked through the gate, trepidatiously approaching the bench to take a seat next to her.

Erin forced a smile. "You startled me." She fidgeted with her tissue to avoid eye contact with him.

Nathan reached over and pressed a finger under her chin, raising her face until their eyes met. "I'm sorry, Erin. I didn't mean to confuse you or make you feel like I was taking advantage of you. I would never want to do that." *Not bad for no rehearsal.* But he didn't need to rehearse anything since he spoke directly from his heart. He scanned her face, trying to read her expression to determine if reconciliation was possible.

Erin raised her hand to meet his finger resting on her chin. She brought his hand down, lacing her fingers with his. "I know. And I'm sorry too, Nate. I know you're not a player, and I shouldn't have said that."

Nathan felt his body relax. He knew there was still so much that needed to be said, but at least she was talking to him and not chasing him out of the garden with a torch or pitchfork. "You don't owe me an apology." He sighed, rubbing a thumb over her hand. "Look, I know our situation is complicated. I also know that I've felt different this week since I've met you. I don't know what the future holds, but I want to figure it out. With you." His voice shook with uncertainty, and he locked eyes with hers to emphasize his last two words.

Erin looked at him with fresh tears forming. Without a word, he wrapped an arm around her shoulders, pulling her in for a hug. She leaned into him, relaxing her body against his embrace. He breathed deeply, memorizing the scent as he placed a protective hand on her head.

Erin pulled back, looking into his eyes. Nathan brushed hair from her face, gently kissing her forehead. He could see her mind working overtime. "Penny for your thoughts?"

She sighed. "It's been a day of mixed emotions."

I can relate.

"I received a letter from someone who wants to buy The Gilded Rose."

Nathan shifted. He waited for her to expound further, but she didn't. "Are you considering the offer?"

"I—I'm not sure."

Nathan studied her. "For what it's worth, I think you're terrific at what you do. I know things have been slow, but with time, it'll pick up. It already is, since we went to Cheshire Moon."

"Thanks, and you're right." Erin twisted the hem of her shirt between two fingers.

Nathan placed a finger under her chin, gently pulling her gaze toward his. "But?"

Erin exhaled. "I got another letter today. A different kind of letter that brought up some memories from the past." She pulled away from him, folding her arms protectively over her chest. "The letter was from an organ transplant department. Apparently, someone received Adam's heart when he died, and they sent me a thank-you note." She shook her head. "It re-opened some old wounds for me, and it's been hard to focus."

Nathan felt the air shift around him, and he cleared his throat. "Where was the letter from?"

"Seattle, coincidentally. I wonder if it's someone you might know, but there was no name or contact information. That's best, I guess. I don't know if it would really help knowing who the person is."

Nathan's heart raced. It couldn't be, could it? The odds he'd received her husband's heart had to be . . . what, a million to one? But something stirred within him. A knowing. Was there such a thing as heart's intuition? Adrenaline coursed through his veins, making him feel nauseous. He needed to see that letter. Needed to be sure.

"Nate, are you okay?"

He nodded. "I think I need some water. Do you need anything?" When she shook her head, he excused himself, promising to return. He couldn't take his mind off the odds, wondering how lucky he felt. But which way would be considered lucky: him having the heart or not having it?

Nathan entered the kitchen and saw a stack of mail on the kitchen table, taunting him to take a peek. He knew not to go seeking answers to questions when he wasn't prepared for the outcome. While this definitely classified as one of those moments, he knew there was nothing he could do to truly prepare for whatever lay ahead.

He took a step toward the table, then stopped. He could hear Frances in his mind telling him it was rude to intrude. Given the circumstances, he felt this was an exception to proper etiquette and manners and took another step forward.

Was he hoping he *did* have her husband's heart or did *not*?

Before he could figure out the answer, his hands were moving through the stack of mail on the table with fervor. His heart leapt into his throat and he forced himself to suck in a breath as his hands uncovered the truth.

There it was. The familiar blue envelope, folded and creased from being carried around with him for almost a year, stared at him from the table. He even recognized a rogue coffee stain from the original Starbucks near Pike's Market during one of his failed attempts to mail it. He'd accidentally spilled some of his dark roast on the envelope and wiped it off with the cuff of his blazer. He thought he'd gotten it all, but the evidence remained.

He needed to sit down.

Stumbling into the chair next to the table, he couldn't tear his eyes away from the letter he'd spent countless hours staring at during his many failed attempts to mail it. Nathan wasn't a man of faith and didn't believe in fate. But how was this possible? Of all the people to receive a heart from, it was Erin's husband. Adam. His suffering gave Nathan a second chance at life.

A first chance at love.

But was any of that even real?

He shook his head, shoving the envelope and letter under the stack. A bead of sweat pooled on his brow, as his (or was it Adam's?) heart pounded in his chest. This was too much. He needed to get out of there.

Nathan jumped as he heard the door from the garden open and shut. He scrambled to his feet, searching for a glass to fill with water.

"Everything okay?" Erin asked.

Nathan shook his head, avoiding eye contact with her. "I'm not feeling too well."

Looking concerned, Erin took a step toward him. "Anything I can do for you?"

You've already done enough. He stepped back, holding out a hand to keep her away. "No, I'm okay. Just need to lie down. The last few days have caught up with me. Talk later?" She nodded reluctantly, and he exited the kitchen, doing his best to avoid eye contact in fear he'd spill his guts right then and there.

Distance. Space. That was what he needed more than anything right now.

*E*rin put away the last of the dishes from breakfast in the kitchen cupboards. Violet had already gotten a head start on the rooms, and the only thing that stood between her and a lukewarm cup of coffee was folding towels from the dryer. But even as she began folding them into a neat stack, she was on edge.

Something felt off.

She couldn't put her finger on it, but when she woke up that morning something had shifted. She reviewed a mental checklist to ensure everything was in place and nothing was missing. She recounted her steps in the dining room, and all the dishes were accounted for. She even checked all the burners on the stove three times, every time confirming they were all off. Maybe she'd grown delirious from not having finished a hot cup of coffee in days. She decided to brew another pot as a process of elimination.

Last night's sleep provided no additional clarity to her on what to do about the offer to purchase the inn. She might have to break down and consult outside sources for insight into her dilemma. Brooke always provided good advice, and besides, that's what friends were for, right? She'd be able to help Erin see things objectively, although Erin anticipated Brooke might be slightly biased on a certain geographic location. She'd hoped Nathan would provide some feedback, but he'd left soon after their sunset reconciliation.

One thing she did feel completely resolved in was her feelings for Nathan. Despite her mind telling her not to get involved, she couldn't deny the stirring in her heart for a man that offered nothing but a vague promise of figuring things out with her. If she were honest with herself, that's about all she could offer in the present moment too. With some uncertainty around her about the inn, she needed to put some puzzle pieces together before the whole picture could take form. She knew Nathan was definitely a piece in her puzzle. She just wasn't sure where or how he'd fit just yet.

It still surprised her how much Nathan had grown to mean to her in the last few days. It made no logical sense, but he'd changed her life the moment he checked in. There was so much about him that reminded her of Adam, including weird phrases he said, the way he'd tenderly kissed her forehead, and the way he'd comforted her yesterday.

Would she always compare every man in her life to Adam? If she had learned anything in the last year or so, it was that nothing in life is guaranteed. Life was too short, too fragile, to let the past hold her back from finding happiness. No doubt, Adam would always hold a special place in her heart, but she was truly ready to embrace the next chapter of her life without him. Possibly with Nathan.

So why couldn't she shake the feeling that something was off?

Violet entered the kitchen, a confused look on her face.

"What is it?" Erin asked.

"I thought Nathan was staying another night."

"He is. Why?"

"It looks like he's gone."

Erin's heart jumped into her throat. Gone? That couldn't be right. "You're sure he's not just gone for the day?"

Violet shook her head. "His room is clear."

Erin felt every fiber of her being screaming *this* was what was off. He'd really left without a word? Without saying goodbye? She couldn't understand, especially after everything they'd shared and experienced together. Although, he'd acted really strange last night, suddenly falling ill after she talked about the letters she'd received. Was he really not feeling well, or did he suddenly have a guilty conscience? Maybe Kendall was right about him after all.

No. She shook her head. She was grasping at straws, her mind assuming the worst. There had to be an explanation. This couldn't be the end. After everything they'd been through together, she knew him better than to just disappear. She was overreacting and assuming the worst. He'd call her later.

Or maybe he wouldn't. Maybe he'd never call again just like Adam never did. After all, her gut had been telling her all morning something was wrong. Fear crept through her veins, making her feel sick to her stomach with the idea of reliving the pain of losing someone she cared for. Her heart couldn't endure that kind of loss a second time.

"I take it you weren't expecting him to check out?" Violet asked.

Erin shook her head, her skin going pale. "Something is wrong. I feel it." She had a thought. His phone number should be listed in her guest information book. She pushed back her chair, knocking it to the ground as she headed toward the book to search for a phone number and answers. She flipped the pages, and there it was. His phone number written in blue ink.

She pulled her cell phone out of her back pocket and dialed, waiting for him to answer. She longed to hear his voice confirm her overreaction to assuming the worst, telling her he'd stepped out for an unexpected errand or some other likely explanation. But when he didn't answer, her pulse raced.

"Any luck?" Violet asked, and Erin shook her head. "I'm sure he's fine."

That made one of them. "I can't shake the feeling he's not." She felt tears forming in her eyes, panic settling in.

"Try him again," Violet said.

Erin dialed his number again, willing Nathan to pick up. She took a deep breath and prayed.

NATHAN SAT in an uncomfortable chair in a stark, sterile room at Harborview Medical Center in Seattle. Bleary eyed, he held onto Frances' hand, willing her to wake up. He swallowed hard. He wasn't ready to lose Frances. She'd been his saving grace his entire life, having been there for him when the two people he trusted the most in his life couldn't. His mind felt deceived. She looked like she was peacefully resting, off in the dreamworlds and not fighting death. Any minute now, she'd groggily rub her eyes and ask him about his trip to San Francisco. She *had* to.

He'd received a call from a nurse last night telling him she'd been admitted after being hit by a car and had been unresponsive. Her vitals were good, and the medical staff assured him it was a matter of time until she woke up. All signs pointed to an eventual full recovery, but her body just needed some additional rest. He hoped they were right.

He didn't hesitate the moment he hung up the phone to pack his things and head straight for the airport. Fortunately, he got the last seat on the last flight out and sped toward the hospital once he landed. He couldn't help feeling overrun with guilt. Had he been in town, he could have taken her wherever she was going. He could have kept her from walking into traffic at the wrong moment, helping her avoid the accident in the first place. But instead, he was off gallivanting with a beautiful woman in California.

Not being there for Frances wasn't the only thing prodding Nathan's guilt. He'd left without a word to Erin. He couldn't help feeling like that was the coward's way out, but he didn't have time to think about much else other than Frances at the time. Although Frances wasn't the only reason he'd left. He needed time after finding the familiar blue envelope on her kitchen table. Hopefully, Erin would understand when he explained himself, whenever he could find the right words.

Too bad Hallmark hadn't come up with a card for the occasion. *Surprise! I have your dead husband's heart.* Maybe disappearing would be the right course of action. Besides, that was something he knew how to do and always did, when the time came for him to move on to another exotic locale in the world. Clean break, no words. That's what worked for him in the past.

Nathan knew he couldn't do that to her, his heart ripping apart at the thought. This was different. Erin wasn't just another fling. He'd never experienced feelings like this before for any other woman in his life. She sparked something in him that he didn't even know was possible. He hadn't been sure if he was even capable of feeling the things he'd felt when he was with her, and she'd proved to him there were still things he didn't know about himself. But he couldn't help wondering if what he'd felt for Erin over the last several days was real. Had he truly fallen for her, or was it a feeling his heart was accustomed to from being in its previous vessel? Maybe it was all fabricated, a residual condition from his secondhand heart.

But he wasn't the only part in the complicated equation. Could Erin feel anything real for him, knowing he had her husband's heart? Maybe she was only drawn to him because he harbored a part of her past, a part of her true love, and she'd sensed it on some level. Even if she said the words he'd hoped to hear, that she cared for *him*, could he believe her? The idea made everything they'd experienced feel contrived and fabricated.

Frances stirred, turning her head to the left side from the right. Nathan's pulse raced as he waited for her eyelids to flutter, revealing deep blue eyes full of warmth and love. But she stayed asleep. He took her movement as a sign she wouldn't be out much longer. He felt hopeful as he brought her knuckles to his lips, kissing them gently.

His phone buzzed in his pocket, the number on his caller ID indicating it was someone calling from Mystic Beach. He knew it was Erin. He knew he should answer. But he couldn't, instead watching the screen flicker to a missed call alert and eventually go black. What would he say to her? He needed to figure that out before he talked to her.

But would he ever find the right words?

His phone buzzed again, the same number coming across his caller ID. He needed to face the inevitable and fumble his way through it. "Hey," he answered.

"Nate?"

His heart fluttered at the sound of her voice and the way she called him Nate.

"Is everything okay?" she asked.

How would he answer that? Nothing was okay, and he was starting to wonder if anything ever would be again.

"Hello?"

"Sorry." He cleared his throat. "I'm here."

"Well, I'm glad to know you're not dead, but why'd you leave?"

"Frances is in the hospital."

She sucked in a breath. "What? What happened?"

He rubbed his forehead. "She was hit by a car and still hasn't woken up."

"Oh, Nate. I'm so sorry."

"That's not all," he forced himself to say. Dead air hung between them. He knew what he had to do, but he cringed before ripping off the Band-Aid.

"Whatever it is, just say it." Her voice shook, and he grimaced. He didn't want to cause her pain and knew she deserved better.

He took a deep breath. "I don't know how else to say it than to just come out with it. I wrote your transplant letter."

Now it was her turn to be quiet. He knew she was still on the other end because he could hear her breathing. He waited for her to respond. Besides, he had a leg up on time to process this atomic bomb, although time hadn't brought him any closer to resolve.

Erin sputtered incomprehensibly before formulating a double question. "What . . . how?"

As silence hung heavy between them, he felt like his chest were being ripped apart. What he'd experienced in the last several days with Erin felt so real to him, and he could tell the feelings were mutual. He was no stranger to knowing when a woman was attracted to him, and Erin was definitely interested. But now that he knew the true source of his heart, he couldn't help thinking that was the only reason she was truly into him. Besides, the two people who he'd trusted and loved the most had discarded him as if he were a carton of old milk. He obviously wasn't enough for them, so how could he be enough for her?

Emotions caught in his throat and tears threatened to

form. He needed to cut things off before they both endured more heartache than necessary. That was the least he could do for her. For them. "I—I have to go."

"Nate, wait."

"I can't," he forced out before ending the call.

15

*E*rin stared at her phone screen as it faded to black, feeling an overwhelming wave of confusion wash over her. Nathan had written the organ donor letter. Nathan harbored Adam's heart. How was that even possible? She'd woken up so sure about her feelings for Nathan, ready to chart their course, one step at a time. But everything changed in a flash, and now she wasn't sure about anything.

"What is it?" Violet asked.

Erin struggled to find the right words to explain the unexplainable. There was no way she could tell Violet what was really going on in her mind. She couldn't make sense of it herself. She opted for a partial truth. "Nathan's aunt is in the hospital."

Violet's eyes grew wide. "Is she alright?"

Another loaded question. Would any of them be alright ever again? Erin needed to process the barrage of questions in her own mind before she could speak about it to anyone. She didn't even understand it herself, so how could she explain the situation to an innocent bystander? Erring on the side of caution, she nodded, although she knew from Violet's expression that she wasn't buying the lame attempts at dodging the subject.

Violet leaned over to give Erin a hug, and Erin, shell-shocked, robotically wrapped an arm around Violet. "It's all going to be okay," Violet soothed, gently rubbing her back.

Erin felt tears forming in her eyes, and she gave Violet a squeeze before pulling away. She scanned the room, suddenly feeling claustrophobic. "I think I need some air. I'll be back." She didn't wait for a response, quickly grabbing her purse and heading out the back door, letting it slam behind her. Fresh air seeped into her lungs as she took a deep breath. She fought the urge to fall to her knees, weak without answers. Weak from the loss of something that had barely taken shape but was still irrefutably real. Her heart ached, the scar tissue holding it together threatening to give way.

She stumbled to the garden, sitting on the bench she'd last shared with Nathan. Where he'd said he wanted to figure out their future together. Where she'd felt her heart truly open for the first time since Adam died. But was anything she'd felt in the last week even remotely true? She wondered if on some level her subconscious knew it was Adam's heart, and she'd fallen right back in love with him. Her grip on reality loosened. She was scared and confused. And solitude wasn't helping her get any closer to making sense of the cruel situation.

Erin needed to get away from the inn. She needed space from the place that harbored fresh memories with Nathan. Clarity had to come from somewhere else. She hopped into her car and turned the engine over. She wound her way down the hill toward downtown on autopilot, heading toward familiar ground for comfort. Being a private person, she wasn't sure how she would attempt to verbalize what had happened, but she knew containing this burden on her own wouldn't provide any help either. She needed her best friend.

At the very least, maybe Brooke had some kind of antidote to her pain.

After she pulled into a parking space behind Batter Up, she got out and locked her car. She hoped to find Brooke when she entered through the back door, but she was nowhere to be found. Erin poked her head through the door to the front of the store to ask Diego, who helped Brooke occasionally at the register. He was busy with a customer but said she'd run over to Denise's.

Erin walked through the bakery to the front door and crossed the street to enter Celestial Books and Brew. Nag champa incense mixed with an Ethiopian roast filled her senses when she walked through the door, and light harp music played from a nearby radio. She saw Brooke and Denise chatting animatedly, Brooke leaning against Denise's front case display.

"Were your ears burning?" Denise smiled. Her dark hair was pulled up in a bun, revealing dangly gold earrings that reflected in the light above. She wore a leather vest over a gauzy white dress, looking every bit the flower child.

"Hey, girl. We were just talking about you," Brooke said warmly. She'd taken the time to do her hair, flowing dark curls grazing her shoulders and upper back. Was Erin mistaken, or was Brooke also wearing makeup?

Both of the other ladies' expressions changed when they assessed Erin, who didn't even pause to give herself a once over before she greeted them. Her emotions would have been impossible to hide anyway. "Is everything okay?" Brooke asked.

Erin shook her head. "I . . . I don't . . ." She struggled to speak, tears forming in the corners of her eyes.

Brooke immediately pulled Erin into a hug. "Shh...let it all go." She stroked the back of Erin's head in a comforting way as Erin gave up the fight in holding back tears, letting them cascade down her face.

"I'll make us some tea." Denise moved behind the front case to make a pot.

"Can you also grab some of those?" Brooke called over her shoulder to Denise, who nodded and grabbed a plate for some of Brooke's cookies.

Erin pulled herself together as Brooke ushered her to a seat at a blue and gold mosaic bistro table near the back of the room. Erin kept her eyes on her hands as they fidgeted on the table, afraid she'd fall apart again if she looked at Brooke's sympathetic expression.

"I'm here to listen when you're ready to talk," Brooke assured, placing a hand on her shoulder.

Erin nodded and focused on steadying her breath. Just being with Brooke made her feel better, and she knew immediately she'd done the right thing by choosing not to be alone. Denise joined them at the table with a pot of tea and a plate of Brooke's cookies.

"I didn't realize we'd need these cookies so soon," Denise said.

"Somehow, I knew we'd need some happiness today." Brooke reached over to pat Erin's fidgeting hands.

"I don't know how you do it." Erin forced a smile with watery eyes.

"And she'll never tell, will you?" Denise said playfully.

Brooke shook her head. "It's a Santos family secret. I wouldn't dare."

Denise rolled her eyes. "It's probably just a placebo."

Brooke shrugged. "Believe what you want."

Denise poured tea into their cups and passed a jar of honey to Erin first. Erin forced herself to steady her hand as she sweetened her mug. She took a sip, drinking in the comfort of warm tea and good friends as she felt her nerves settle. She appreciated the fact that neither woman badgered her into speaking, giving her the space to process how to share what was on her mind. Maybe it would be easier to start with the tangible topic first. "I received a letter from an investor who wants to buy The Gilded Rose."

Brooke dropped the honey spoon in the jar. "What?"

"Who?" Denise asked.

"Some guy from Chicago. He made a generous offer."

Brooke shifted in her seat. "I wasn't aware you wanted to sell the inn."

"I wasn't. I mean, I'm not," Erin corrected.

"You sure?" Denise asked, eyeing her suspiciously.

Erin paused, looking at her friends. Despite the challenges she'd faced in the last couple of months taking over the inn and the constant struggle with the feeling of inadequacy of living up to Nancy's legacy, she couldn't help feeling like she belonged there. She certainly no longer belonged in her old life and wouldn't turn back to it even when presented with an opportunity to do so. The multiple zeroes in the offer was more than generous and would allow Erin to start over anywhere. But no amount of money could replace the relationships she'd built since returning to her hometown.

Even with the knowledge that something heavy was on her mind, neither Brooke nor Denise looked at her with pity. She hadn't realized it before that moment, but Mystic Beach was her home. She didn't want to leave.

"Yes, I'm sure of it now," Erin said.

Brooke relaxed. "Good. Now you can have one of my cookies." She passed the plate to Erin, who took a bite of the shortbread cookie. Her eyes closed as rosemary danced on her tongue, a wave of happiness washing over her. "Better?" Brooke asked, and Erin nodded.

Denise studied Erin. "That's not all, though, is it?"

Erin looked at Denise, wondering how she was able to

intuit things when Erin thought she had mastered her poker face. "No."

"You don't have to pretend anything with us, you know," Denise said. "We'll never judge you." Brooke nodded in agreement.

"I know." Erin sighed. "It just doesn't make any sense to me, that's all." Brooke and Denise both waited for Erin to continue. She took a deep breath and told them about the transplant letter and who wrote it. When she finished, she looked at both women, who stared at her as they processed the burden she'd unloaded.

"So, Nathan has your husband's heart?" Brooke asked, wrinkling her forehead.

"What are the odds?" Denise said.

"I know, right?" Erin said. "I can't believe it, either."

"You should probably play the lotto," Brooke joked, obviously trying to lighten the mood. "But seriously, how does that make you feel?"

Erin looked at the tea swirling in her mug as she stirred in a little more honey. "I'm not sure. I guess I'm still having a hard time understanding it. Makes me wonder if I've fallen for Nathan because on some level he reminded me of Adam."

Brooke perked up. "You fell for Nathan?"

Erin nodded. It was the first time she'd said the words out loud, and she felt partial relief in admitting her true feelings. She'd planned to tell Nathan first, but that was quickly derailed. "But now…"

"Well, in a way it's kind of sweet, don't you think?" Denise said. Both Erin and Brooke looked at her with confusion. "I mean, Adam's heart found its way back to you."

Denise's words hit Erin like a Mack truck. Her bottom lip quivered as she fought tears again. When she put it like that, it was utterly romantic. But it didn't make anything less complicated.

"Where is Nathan now?" Brooke asked.

"In the hospital in Seattle. His aunt, not him," Erin clarified when shock spread across Brooke's face.

"When is he coming back?" Brooke asked.

"I don't think he is," Erin said ruefully. "It's probably for the best."

"Something tells me you haven't seen the last of him," Denise said.

Erin wasn't sure if she wanted that to be true or not. She needed time to process. Time to figure out what she wanted. It dawned on her that the one person she really needed to talk to was no longer alive, but she'd have to accept the next best thing. It was the only way she'd be able to finally move forward, with or without Nathan.

NATHAN'S HEART ached with guilt from ending the call so abruptly. He felt embarrassed having displayed such poor manners in front of the woman who raised him better than that. *Wake up and tell me off*, he silently challenged Frances as he watched her sleeping peacefully. This couldn't be the end for them.

Listening to the steady rhythm of machines beeping and whooshing gave him hope that Frances would, in fact, wake up. He wasn't ready to lose her. Even the thought of that left him feeling empty inside. Frances had been the only woman he'd ever truly loved, the one who'd saved him when his mother thought he was too much to handle. The one who loved him in spite of his shortcomings, both physical and emotional. The idea of never getting to talk to her again, see the sparkle in her eye as she looked at him with pride and hear her attempt at a stern voice when she called him on his crap, left him feeling a form of panic.

Besides, Nathan needed a healthy dose of reality from time to time, and Frances always served him exactly that. She'd been everything to him: a mother, a best friend, and his only confidante. He shook his head. *Please don't take her away from me yet*, he pleaded, looking toward the ceiling. "I'll do anything," he said out loud.

"Will you?" Frances strained in a raspy tone.

Relief swept over Nathan as he realized he hadn't imagined Frances speaking. She was awake. His body trembled as he fought back tears. "You're alive."

"Of course I am." She shifted, wincing from pain as she tried to find a comfortable position.

Nathan gripped her hand firmly, bringing it to his lips to place a tender kiss on her knuckles. "You scared me to death." He held her cold fingers against his face. She'd never looked so beautiful in her white and blue hospital gown and sallow complexion with expressions of pain from coming back to life.

"I'm afraid you're stuck with me for a little longer, kiddo." She coughed.

Anticipating her need, Nathan reluctantly let go of her hand and grabbed a nearby bottle of water. He twisted off the cap and held the bottle for her while she gulped desperately. She placed her cold, boney fingers on his arm, indicating she'd had enough, and he placed the bottle on a table.

"Where were you this time before…?" She trailed off.

"Mystic Beach." He brushed salt and pepper fringe back from her forehead.

"Weren't you supposed to be at a conference?" she asked, remembering his travel schedule.

"I was, but I also spent a few days in Mystic Beach as a favor to their mayor," he continued, anticipating her next question. "It's a sweet little town. I think you'd really like it."

"Oh? What's so special about it?"

Erin. He paused, at a loss for words as he remembered their conversation while Frances was still sleeping.

"Nate?" she pressed.

"Well, I think they might have the best lobster roll I've ever had." He quickly changed the subject. "It was a nice way to ease into the conference. My panel discussion went well, by the way."

"And how was the meeting with the execs?"

"Fine." He summarized the meeting and the fact that Coco said a contract was imminent.

Her face brightened. "That's great news. "Where do you fly out to first?"

Nathan shifted. "I'm not sure if I'll be accepting it, but none of that matters right now."

Frances frowned. "Why? And don't say because of me." When Nathan didn't say anything, Frances rolled her eyes. "You can't put your life on hold for me, Nate."

"I'm not."

"Yes, you are. Don't lie."

Nathan held her hand. "Now is not the time."

Frances let go of his hand, holding hers up as an indication for him to stop talking. "I need to say something." She took a deep breath, apparently finding the strength to say what was on her mind. "I know it's just been you and me for a long time, and you know I love you like my own. But obviously, I'm not going to be here forever."

Nathan peered into her crystal blue eyes, feeling the fear of losing her all over again. Emotions caught in his throat. "You scared me," he admitted.

Frances nodded. "I know, and that's what scares *me.*" When Nathan looked at her with confusion, she continued. "I can't be the only woman in your life anymore, Nate. I want you to find a woman to love. You have so much to give to someone."

Nathan leaned back in his chair, crossing his arms. He wasn't sure what to say to Frances, who meant everything to him. She was the only person who never abandoned him, and he could always count on her. And perhaps that was a lot of pressure to put on someone who was closer to death than he cared to admit. There was no denying it now, seeing her horizontal in a hospital bed with tubes and wires connected to different parts of her. Death would come, eventually, and what would he do without her?

"You have a beautiful heart, and you should share it with someone other than me. I want you to find a woman to love and love her with total abandon. I know you will feel sad when I die, but I don't want you to feel like you've lost everything. Find someone to share your life with. Settle down, stop running. Preferably *before* I die," she added, smiling.

Nathan fought back tears. He swallowed the emotions threatening to spill over. The woman he felt he could love with total abandon came with complications. Was it possible for them to get past the fact that he was the new host for her husband's heart? He always felt like he'd been living in the shadows of how much more he could have been as a child in order to keep his mom from leaving him. He'd always felt inadequate. Incomplete. If only he wasn't born broken, perhaps he could have been enough to love.

And now that he'd found a woman who made him feel more complete than anyone he'd ever met, he couldn't help wondering if he would always be living in her dead husband's shadow. The world had a cruel sense of humor, and Nathan was tired of feeling like a constant punch line.

"What is it?" Frances asked.

"Nothing," he lied.

"Nate, come on. I know you better than anyone. Spit it out."

He sighed, running a hand through his hair. "It's so...I'm not sure how to describe it."

Frances eyed him. "You've met someone." At his surprised look, she continued. "I can see it now. Who?"

How did she always know everything? "Her name is Erin."

"Erin," she said slowly, as if testing how the name felt on her lips. "And how did you two meet?"

"She runs a bed and breakfast in Mystic Beach."

She nodded. "Go on."

"She has this...infectious smile. And she's super smart, and her eyes...they're this deep green, and she's stunningly beautiful and has no idea." His face lit up talking about her, then changed when he remembered why he could never have her.

"But...?" Frances urged.

"Well, her husband died a little over a year ago in an accident. It just so happens he was an organ donor." He paused, waiting to see if Frances might put two and two together.

"Okay..."

"And his heart was donated to someone in Seattle." He gave her a piercing glance, waiting for recognition to take hold. "Someone in this room."

The proverbial light bulb flashed. "Oh! Wow," she said, followed by a cacophony of mumbles and facial expressions as her mind chewed on the information. She paused, finally reaching resolve. "Okay, so what?"

Nathan raised an eyebrow. "So what? I have her dead husband's heart. Don't you think that's...weird?"

Frances considered his point of view. "No, I think it's remarkable and, dare I say, romantic." When Nathan opened his mouth to counter, she continued. "What's a heart? It's, what, less than a pound of muscle, tissue, and blood? The heart in your chest does not make up who you are. It's the heart of you, your soul, that makes you *you*."

Nathan felt like the wind had been knocked out of him. He marveled at how Frances' words had the ability to sucker punch him when he least expected it, and this was no exception. "Okay, you have a point." Would Erin be able to see things the same way? Was he admitting he agreed?

She grabbed his hand. "If you love this woman, don't let the heart in your chest keep you from her. True love is hard to find, and you should grab her and never let go."

His brow furrowed. "I'm not sure if I *love* her. Those are strong words."

"You're right. But I think you owe it to yourself to go find out for sure."

"Knock, knock." A man in a white lab coat entered the room. "Glad to see you're awake." The doctor proceeded to examine Frances, asking her to tell him the date, who the current president was, and to verify that he was holding up two fingers.

Nathan felt his body relax at no longer being the one under Frances's microscope, but he definitely had his own internal examination to conduct. He'd certainly have time to think about everything, since he'd be canceling his trip to Jamaica. He couldn't leave Frances in the hospital alone. Taking on the role of caring for the woman who raised him would hopefully bring him the clarity he desperately needed.

16

*E*rin drove the familiar route toward a hill overlooking the bustling city. She'd rolled down her windows to drink in the sun as it peeked through the clouds, hoping its rays would provide the warmth she needed for this cold conversation. She found a parking spot near a bigleaf maple tree, its leaves barely brushed with the impending signature of autumn's light gold. Nearby redbud and dogwood trees stood prominently overlooking the park, with multiple bouquets left for loved ones adding pops of color against the grey stone markers. As she walked past rows of the dearly departed, she couldn't help feeling like something had changed. Everything in the park was as she remembered it, but it felt different somehow. She shook her head, feeling guilty for coming to this sacred place empty-handed. But just her, as she was, would have to do.

"Hello, handsome," she greeted the headstone which poorly summarized a life: Adam James Pedersen; Beloved Husband and Son. His resting place felt as familiar as a worn-in pair of jeans, hugging her curves perfectly. Erin closed her eyes, her mind almost tricking her into the warm comfort of Adam pulling her into his embrace. She often came here to talk to him when she missed him or when she needed to talk to someone who truly knew her. Despite the one-sided nature of their conversations, Adam still provided solace when she truly needed it.

"Let me clean you up first." Her fingertips traced blades of grass as she knelt beside the site and removed a few stray pieces covering the headstone. Assessing her work, she felt satisfied. "Much better." She forced a smile as she settled down and crossed her legs to get comfortable.

"I'm sorry I haven't been here in a while." She used to visit him every Sunday afternoon when she lived in the city. She'd bring a cup of coffee and tell him everything going on in her life, often ending in tears with how much she missed him. But when she moved to Mystic Beach a few months ago, her visits became less frequent. The distance was partially responsible, but she also felt like she'd been treading water ever since she took over the inn. It was hard to get away.

"I received an offer this week from someone who wants to purchase the inn." She pulled at a blade of grass, playing with it between her fingers. "I don't know what to do, and I wish you could tell me. I'm not sure if I'm truly cut out to be an innkeeper, but I feel like I'd be letting Nancy down if I threw in the towel. If you see her, tell her I say hello. I hope she's proud of me for what I've done so far."

She paused, appreciating the view from Adam's resting place. She'd specifically chosen a plot with a view of the entire bay area, and everything seemed to blur from moving quickly from her vantage point. At the same time, things came into sharper focus on higher ground. She swallowed the lump forming in her throat as she prepared to say what else was on her mind.

"I remember we talked briefly about our wishes for one another if either of us went first. I know you told me you wanted me to share my heart with someone else and not hold back in fear of losing love again." Her voice shook, and she took a deep breath. "As much as I wish you were still here, I know you'd want me to move on with my life. I'm trying, taking things one day at a time. But it's still so hard."

She paused. "Adam, I miss you so much." Tears welled in her eyes. "It's funny, actually, a guest came to the inn this week who received a heart transplant over a year ago. Apparently, you were the donor." Emotions caught in her throat, forcing her to pause. "It's like a part of you came back to me." A tear slowly streamed down her cheek. She couldn't keep them at bay anymore and allowed the tears to fall as she felt every emotion from love to heartbreak all over again.

Erin's thoughts wandered to Nathan. She thought about how he made her laugh, how protective he was, and how his very presence made her insides melt to goo. The tender way he framed her face in his hands as he kissed her with passion, and his strong lips sparked her entire body aflame. There was a lot about Nathan that reminded her of Adam, but he was definitely a different person. She loved the things about Nathan that were uniquely him.

That's when it hit her. She was in love with Nathan. She loved *him*, not the fact that he had Adam's heart. She loved his *true* heart—the very essence of him. But things would never work between them. Despite their similarities and the undeniable chemistry, they were two people leading very different lives. He was about to be a television star and thrived in the spotlight. She wanted nothing to do with that. And besides, she didn't think he could ever get past the fact that his heart had previously belonged to her husband.

From what little she knew about organ donations and transplants, the recipients were finally given their shot at living a full life. She'd read articles in the past that made her clutch her own heart about people receiving eyes from a donor and being able to see clearly for the first time in their lives. Or someone who received a kidney from a loved one in order to stay alive. What a beautiful act of service organ donation was when clearly, the departed no longer required use of their fully functioning organs but could provide life to someone else.

So what if parts of his body, the vehicle he used to express his love and leave his mark on this world, were harvested and given to other people? An organ, a piece of flesh, does not define who a person is. She believed Adam's soul, his true essence, lived on in Heaven. He was no longer there, so why was she desperately holding onto the past, pretending like he still was?

"I appreciate that part of you did come back to me, for even the briefest amount of time. You showed me love in countless ways when you were alive, and even in death, you continue to teach me about love. Adam, you still surprise me, and I will always love you. I'll never forget you, and I may still talk to you from time to time, but I know you'd want me to move on." She pulled a tissue from her pocket and dabbed the corners of her eyes, thankful she'd skipped the mascara that day. "And I *want* to move on too."

A warm breeze tickled her skin as a feather landed on her knee. Adam had always pointed out feathers to her everywhere they went. If he found one while they were walking down the street, he'd pick it up and hand it to Erin. "Feathers are good luck," he'd say, and she usually rolled her eyes. She held the avian gift of love in her hand and smiled, looking toward the sky with appreciation at his approving gesture. "Thank you, baby. For everything."

NATHAN STALLED, not ready to say goodbye.

He double-checked to make sure Frances had everything and anything imaginable within arm's reach. He knew leaving her after the accident was inevitable, but it felt harder this time. Of course, her accident had something to do with it, but this particular trip felt different. He was leaving her to meet up with Coco, Jeff, and Simon to discuss pilot filming for Wander-Lust Abroad, the working title for his new show.

He'd quickly signed the documents about a month ago, too consumed with taking care of Frances to pay much attention to the detail and wanting to check one more item off his to-do list that day. He'd kept putting off the meeting, his excuse that Frances wasn't ready to be alone yet. But Coco told him it was either now or they were going to move forward with their second choice, the well-traveled and very handsome Paul Fitzgerald, whom he had drinks with a couple of times at TravelCon. Knowing Paul was the backup plan sparked Nathan's competitive drive. He knew he'd make a better host than that sleaze ball.

"Nate, I'm fine. You need to go. Your plane takes off in less than two hours," Frances said. She'd been so lucky with her accident. For being hit by a car, she'd only fractured one hip, broke two ribs, and significantly bruised her ego. Her age certainly didn't help matters, but she was a tough old bird and determined not to let that car get the best of her. She'd been sent home from the hospital a few weeks ago, and Nathan dove headfirst into caregiving for the woman who had shown him so much love throughout his life. Being of service to her gave him a newfound sense of purpose. It was his turn to return to favor, and he'd accepted the challenge with open arms. "Sherri said she'd look in on me, so you don't need to worry about anything other than your meeting," she reminded him. Sternly.

He paced, looking around the living room for anything

out of place, trying his best to anticipate any need she might possibly have between now and whenever Sherri, Frances' neighbor, showed up later that afternoon. He eyed her refillable water bottle with suspicion. "Looks like you might need more water."

Frances rolled her eyes. "Nate, I've taken two sips. You're being ridiculous. While I appreciate all your doting in the last few weeks, you need to go. I'm fine, and Sherri will be here around three. I think I can occupy myself until then."

Nathan paused. "I'm going to refill it to be sure." He picked up her water bottle and refilled it in the kitchen.

"Are you nervous about this meeting or something?" Frances hollered from the living room.

"No, I'm fine." Nathan should be excited at the prospect of starting filming for a television show. It was his lifelong dream, and he'd built everything toward this pinnacle moment. But as he kept repeating that he was fine, he believed it less and less, and he suspected Frances was catching on too. Even *he* wasn't buying into it anymore, the words empty and trite. However, he kept repeating them to avoid admitting to himself that something was missing. When he allowed himself to stop and think, he suspected what it was. But that wasn't an option, and he knew it.

His dreams about Erin had intensified since spending time with her in Mystic Beach, which felt like a cruel joke his subconscious was playing on him. She was literally his dream girl, and he'd never have her. They hadn't spoken since their last conversation when Frances was in the hospital. He'd looked at his phone, his thumb hovering over the call button on her contact record several times, but he never dialed. He wasn't sure what to say or what could be said.

"*Fine* is becoming my least favorite word."

Nathan handed her a water bottle filled to the brim, looking over her surroundings one more time.

"Nate, cut it out. I'm fine," she said, swatting his leg.

"How come when you say it I'm supposed to believe you, but you don't believe me when I say it?" He crossed his arms.

"Because I truly am fine but you're not, and I think you need to go to California to be sure."

He paused, immediately flashing on Mystic Beach and enjoying the sunset with Erin in the garden at the inn. If only he had one of her friend's courage cookies…he shook the thought away. Frances was probably talking about Los Angeles anyway, and he knew he was already pushing it on making his flight on time. He needed to go.

"Nate, if you don't go right now, I will get up from this chair and kick your ass." They both knew that was an empty threat, but he got the point. He gave in, leaning over to kiss her on the cheek, and promised to call once he'd settled into his hotel in Los Angeles.

"Say hello to Coco for me," Frances called over her shoulder.

Nathan pulled up the handle on his carry-on suitcase and rolled out, locking the door behind him. He'd called a car to take him to the airport, and thankfully, traffic was surprisingly light for the dreaded trek down I-5 toward SeaTac. His driver, an older Indian man, played classical music in the background and gripped the steering wheel at ten and two. He avoided eye contact and conversation with Nathan, who had been hoping to make polite small talk with a stranger to avoid thinking about a certain beautiful blonde again, but no luck. Instead, he reviewed his emails from Coco for the third time, re-reading the itinerary for their meetings with the network.

When they arrived, he pulled his suitcase from his silent companion's trunk and gave him a cash tip. He wheeled through the sliding doors and found the nearest televisions to review departures to be sure his flight was still on time, dodging passengers as they briskly walked toward their destinations.

Nathan noticed a blonde woman walking toward him from the corner of his eye. "There you are," the beauty said, and his heart caught in his throat. He turned toward her, realizing belatedly that she'd been talking to a man in a Burberry coat nearby. The man held out his arms and she leapt into his embrace. He spun her around a few times, kissing her passionately. "I missed you," she murmured, as they smiled widely before kissing each other again.

Nathan forced his attention away, suddenly feeling uncomfortable in his voyeurism. But that wasn't the only thing he felt. He wished that blonde were Erin, and he longed to be the guy in the Burberry coat, wrapping his arms around her and never letting go.

Frances's words echoed in his mind. *You need to go to California to be sure*. It was time for him to be honest. He *wasn't* fine. In fact, nothing had been fine since he'd left Erin, and he knew he'd never be fine again without her. He'd felt his whole life like a part of him was missing. It hit him that the part of him that had been missing was much more than just having a faulty heart full of complications. The first time he'd felt whole in his entire life wasn't right after his surgery. It was after he met Erin.

And so what if he had her husband's heart? Frances was right; it was just an organ made of muscle, tissue, and blood. That organ did not constitute who he was. He was much more than his physical heart. His true heart, the essence of him, beat strongly for Erin, and he could no longer deny it. After all, it was Erin who'd brought him back to life, not her husband's heart.

But what could he do about it? He had signed a contract saying he would spend the next few months filming the first season of his travel show across the globe. Coco told him he'd pushed his luck too hard with putting off this meeting as long as he had. As it stood now, they'd already be jeopardizing the launch date if they didn't start filming next week. His time was up. He was out of favors. Everything he'd worked so hard for was his for the taking. He just needed to board his flight to California.

Nathan scanned the rest of the departures, resolved in what he had to do. There was another flight to California scheduled to take off ten minutes earlier. He took a deep breath and headed toward security. If he hurried, he just might make it.

The big day was finally here.

The Gilded Rose was filled to the brim with a buzz in the air from a small army setting up for what would be the first of many weddings in the garden. Erin tried her best to remember to breathe as she double and triple checked that everything was in place. Blurs of people rushed past her, setting up chairs in the garden, extra tables in the dining room, and a place for cards and gifts by the front door. It warmed her heart to see the inn filled with so many people excited to celebrate the love between two people she'd grown fond of since moving back to Mystic Beach. It didn't hurt they'd already agreed to allow her to use some of their photography for special event marketing for the inn, either. Although, she didn't expect anything less from two very supportive people.

Marco paced in the garden in his black tux, the sun reflecting off the beads of sweat pooling at his brow, while Elise got ready in the honeymoon suite upstairs. Erin watched him from the dining room as he mumbled to himself, glancing down periodically at an index card in his hand. He must be rehearsing his vows.

Erin handed him a napkin. "Don't forget to breathe." She wondered who needed the reminder more; her or Marco?

He emphatically took it and dabbed his forehead. "Thanks." He smiled. "How does she look? Think I could sneak up there for a quick glance?"

Erin playfully patted his arm. "No peeking." They both chuckled. "You'll see her soon enough."

"I've been waiting my whole life for this woman." Emotions caught in his throat.

Erin felt the pangs of her own love she'd waited her whole life for, thinking of Nath—er, Adam. She'd been doing that quite a lot lately. She knew Adam was an intricate part of her past and felt resolved in the fact that Nathan was her future. However, the future never called. Being a modern woman who didn't feel the need to follow old traditions, Erin had picked up her phone to dial his number several times but could never follow through. She kept hearing Denise's words echo in her mind: *If he wants you, he'll call you.* It was in a book she'd read; not for book club, obviously.

Erin had become a regular at the Friday Eve Book Club. She'd forged strong bonds with all the ladies, who helped her feel like she belonged in Mystic Beach again. They'd been a huge part of the life she'd built for herself, and she liked this new version of normalcy. After much deliberation, she'd turned down the offer to purchase The Gilded Rose. Mystic Beach was her home, and even though she had a bit of a rough start, she was finding her own way outside of Nancy's shadow. She imagined her aunt would be very proud of the partnerships she'd formed with several local business owners and that bookings were up as a result. Erin had started beefing up her special events portfolio, hoping to host more weddings. Perhaps Nancy knew all along that she had the right head for business to truly make her vision a reality for the inn. At least, that's what Erin hoped.

A white van with the words Batter Up painted on the side drove up, pulling around toward the back. Brooke had arrived with the wedding cake. Erin excused herself from Marco to greet her friend and help bring in the two-tier lemon chiffon cake covered in white icing and fondant irises.

"Thanks, girl." Brooke was slightly breathless. "It's been a day already. I almost forgot the secret ingredient."

"You're never going to tell me what that is, are you?" Erin asked as they gingerly placed the cake on its designated table.

"I have a feeling I know what it is." The male voice came from behind them.

Erin turned and felt like the wind had been knocked out of her.

It was Nathan. In the flesh.

She'd rehearsed this moment many times over the last few weeks in her mind, but no amount of mental gymnastics prepared her for reality. She felt dumbfounded, completely at a loss for words. And her speechlessness had nothing to do with the fact that he looked good. *Damn* good.

When she finally picked up her jaw from the floor, she uttered a very eloquent, "What are you doing here?"

"It's—" Nathan started.

"No!" Brooke held up her hand to stop him from saying the ingredient out loud. She motioned with her hand for him to whisper it in her ear, and he obliged. After he pulled away, Brooke nodded. "How'd you figure it out?"

"I knew it the first time I tasted those cookies in the kitchen the night we had tea, Erin." His blue-grey eyes locked on hers, crumbling her resolve. "I knew because it was the one thing that had been missing from my life until I met you."

Still processing the fact that Nathan stood before her, let

alone the sweet words he'd just said, Erin's mind flashed back to their last conversation. His disappearance. His heart. His aunt. "What about Frances?"

"She's fine," he said, chuckling.

"What's so funny?"

Nathan shook his head. "Inside joke. But you know what, *I'm* not fine. And I'm finally admitting it. I kept trying to convince myself that I was, but I'm not. I was stupid for running and even dumber for not calling." He took a step toward her, and Erin saw Brooke walk away in her periphery to give them privacy.

Erin felt an overwhelming urge to leap into his arms, but she pushed it away. Just because he was there didn't change the fact that their lives were completely different. Time hadn't changed that. "What about your show and your travel schedule?"

"I just blew off the meeting with Jeff and Simon because I couldn't stop thinking about you. I don't want to spend another minute of my life without you." He took a step forward and paused, only inches of space between them. The electricity of his proximity was palpable. He must have felt it too because he swallowed hard before saying the next words. "Erin, I think I love you."

Erin's heart jumped into her throat, bursting aflame in total bliss. It was everything she'd hoped to hear from him and everything she felt too. "I love you too," she said breathlessly, closing the gap between them.

Nathan's face brightened. "You do?"

Erin nodded. "Yes, and not because of your heart here," she said, placing a hand gently on his chest. "But for your real heart. Who you are, Nate."

He didn't give her a chance to finish saying anything else as he framed her face in his hands and claimed her mouth with his. Her heart set ablaze, melding with its other half that had finally returned. Her lips parted, inviting his tongue to dance with hers, finding a rhythm uniquely theirs. She ran her fingers over the back of his neck, lightly tickling his hairline as she pulled him even closer, feeling every strong muscle in his body against hers.

A male cleared his throat, breaking them from their spell. "If you don't mind, I think we're about ready to start." Marco nodded his head toward the garden.

Nathan reluctantly let go of Erin. They'd have to finish their reunion later. He approached Marco, shaking his hand. "Congratulations," he beamed. "I was thinking about a lot of things over on the flight here, and I have a question for you. Are you still looking to fill your travel ambassador position?"

Marco looked surprised. "Yes, as a matter of fact. Nothing's been finalized with the guy Elise had in mind. Why?"

"Well, how about on Monday I buy you lunch, and we can talk about why you should consider me for the role?"

"Great. But you know we want whoever takes the role to live here full-time."

"I thought you might say that." Nathan brought Erin's hand to his lips, tenderly kissing her knuckles. "I have no intention of going anywhere."

Marco smiled. "Fantastic. I look forward to continuing the conversation next week. But in the meantime, mind if I go get my girl?"

Nathan didn't pull his gaze from Erin. "Not at all."

Marco walked toward the flower-covered trellis in the garden, awaiting his bride-to-be. Nathan helped Erin usher their guests to find seats, and Brooke ascended the stairs to notify Elise it was time. Before they took their seats in the back row, Erin grabbed Nathan's arm and pulled him aside. "You really mean that? You're...staying?"

Nathan pushed a strand of hair behind her ear, and her body trembled from his tender touch. "If you'll have me."

She nodded. "I want nothing more."

He kissed her forehead before pulling her body against his, wrapping his arms around her as they watched their two friends become one in matrimony.

EPILOGUE

*T*he evening was perfect.

Nathan and Erin wandered along a trail, hiking a nearby cliffside to find a good spot to watch the remainder of the sunset and the impending moonrise. Erin said she'd hiked the path many times before, but Nathan grew more skeptical with every step they took. Besides, there wasn't much of a path to speak of, and he was certain she'd gotten them lost. However, he didn't care, because he hadn't felt lost since he'd returned to her.

He had been living in Mystic Beach for three months but still went back to Seattle regularly to look in on Frances. He kept telling her the California sun would do her a lot of good, but she brushed him off, mumbling something about her blood being too thick to handle the heat. She always quickly changed the subject when he reminded her Northern California wasn't too warm, which made him smile. He figured it was just a matter of time until he wore her down enough to join them.

Coco had taken the news pretty hard when Nathan told her he was passing on the opportunity with Jeff and Simon.

He knew she'd been looking forward to that commission check, and he'd offered to pay her for her time. She'd declined and said she was genuinely happy that he'd found love for the first time in his life. When she pitched the idea of incorporating Erin into the show, he chuckled. That would go over like a lead balloon. But if he were being honest, he'd grown comfortable when he finally put his suitcase away in Mystic Beach. Besides, he realized local politics came with its own set of challenges as the new travel ambassador on the city council. He still maintained his blog but focused on micro-tourism for Mystic Beach and the surrounding bay area. With his shirt on, of course. He often paused in amazement at how quickly his life had changed for the better once he'd stood still long enough.

The sun slowly began its descent, the sky colored with pink and purple ribbons wrapping around the last traces of daylight. Night began to cloak the city in darkness, the stars blinking to life. The moon poked its head above the horizon, preparing to rise.

"Come on. Not that much further," Erin said. She claimed to know the best spot to watch a moonrise in Mystic Beach, and Nathan gave her a hard time for holding out on him this entire time. He told her the bar was already set really high when compared to their view from the garden, but she assured him this was different. Magical.

"You said that a mile back," he said, breathing hard.

Erin turned, smiling as she held out her hand for him to grab. "I promise we're almost there."

He took her hand as they walked along the cliffside, admiring Erin's beauty as she turned to smile at him periodically while they made their ascent. The whole climb had a familiarity to it, and it finally dawned on him.

He'd dreamt about this moment multiple times. Every

detail impeccably matched, from her warm hand and bright smile to the purple needle grass gently tickling his legs.

He stopped, letting go of her hand. Reality hit him hard. Was his subconscious trying to tell him something the whole time? *This* was the moment. He knew it with absolute certainty. He dug a hand in his pocket, his fingers tracing a black velvet box he'd been carrying around for at least a month. "This is it," he whispered, adrenaline coursing through his veins.

Erin's brow wrinkled. "What's wrong?" When Nathan didn't say anything, she added, "I promise we're almost there."

Nathan swallowed hard, his nerves almost getting the best of him. "I love you."

Erin smiled. "I know. I love you too. But let's keep going—"

Nathan shook his head, holding up a hand for her to stop talking. "Hang on." He took a deep breath, his heart pounding. "Wow, I'm so nervous." He forced a smile, attempting to break the tension.

Erin gave him the time and space he needed to process his next words, giving him a confused yet encouraging look.

"From the moment I met you, I knew you were different. You have a way of making me feel completely relaxed in being myself. You accept me for who I am, and I'm so grateful I found you."

Erin's face flushed. "Me too, Nate." She took his hand. "You're so easy to love. Life works in mysterious ways sometimes, and despite the unconventional circumstances in how we met, I wouldn't change anything. Not one bit. You mean the world to me."

His pulse pounded in his ears. "I have been carrying this around in my pocket for about a month now, waiting for the right moment, the perfect place, to finally do this." He knelt down, taking the velvet black box from his pocket. His hands shook as he opened it to reveal a ring with three radiant diamonds. "I bought this ring as a symbol of our past, which brought us together in the present. You're everything to me, Erin, and I'm hoping you'll do me the honor of being my future. My wife. Will you marry me?"

Erin placed a hand over her mouth as tears streamed down her face. Her shock quickly melted, and she smiled, an emphatic yes escaping her lips. She leapt into his arms, and he kissed her deeply, passionately, as relief swept over him. They both smiled and kissed again. Their kiss never tasted so sweet as tears of joy streamed down their faces.

"I can't believe it." Erin's voice shook. "You're mine? Forever?"

Nathan pulled away, wiping the tears from her delicate cheeks. She'd never looked more beautiful, and his heart beat steadily, happily, knowing she'd soon be his wife. Everything in his life had led him to this moment, to this perfect woman, and he felt tremendously blessed. Love was so much more than he'd imagined it could be, and Erin made it possible for him. He nodded, pushing hair from her face as it billowed in the breeze. "Forever sounds perfect to me."

ABOUT THE AUTHOR

Roxanne Hensley is the author of Women's Fiction and Romance with happily ever afters and a hint of magical realism. Always a storyteller, she earned a Bachelor's Degree in Creative Writing from Florida State University. When she's not writing, she spends her time reading one of the hundreds of books on her Kindle, shredding the air guitar, quoting movie lines and lyrics, quilting, singing when she thinks no one is listening, or binge watching Netflix. She lives in Austin, Texas with her partner, Dwight, and two cats, Sookie and Gandalf.

To find out more about Roxanne and be the first to know about new releases, sign up for her newsletter on her official website: www.roxannehensley.com

Made in the USA
Columbia, SC
12 June 2020